The Secret of the Golden Flower

A Nicki Haddon
Mystery

The Secret
of the
Golden Flower

CAROLINE STELLINGS

Second Story Press

Library and Archives Canada Cataloguing in Publication

Stellings, Caroline, 1961-, author
The secret of the golden flower / by Caroline Stellings.

"A Nicki Haddon mystery".
Issued in print and electronic formats.
ISBN 978-1-927583-63-0 (pbk.).—ISBN 978-1-927583-68-5 (epub)

I. Title.

PS8587.T4448S43 2015   jC813'.6   C2014-908147-2

C2014-908148-0

Edited by Marianne Ward
Designed by Melissa Kaita
Cover photo © iStockphoto

Printed and bound in Canada

Second Story Press gratefully acknowledges the support of the Ontario Arts Council and the Canada Council for the Arts for our publishing program. We acknowledge the financial support of the Government of Canada through the Canada Book Fund.

ONTARIO ARTS COUNCIL
CONSEIL DES ARTS DE L'ONTARIO
an Ontario government agency
un organisme du gouvernement de l'Ontario

Canada Council   Conseil des Arts
for the Arts   du Canada

Published by
SECOND STORY PRESS
20 Maud Street, Suite 401
Toronto, ON M5V 2M5
www.secondstorypress.ca

For Mildred Wirt Benson and Harriet Stratemeyer Adams
for showing me just how far a female's capabilities can take her

Chapter One

"So where *is* the spy school, Fenwick?" asked Nicki. "Downtown?"

The butler looked from side to side. "Not spy school," he replied in a whisper. "We in the Secret Intelligence Service refer to it as the 'non-field training headquarters.'"

"Non-field?"

"Let's just say that whereas your kung fu teachers have shown you how to knock someone out—"

"Only in self-defense, Fenwick."

"I see," he said. "Well then, whereas your martial arts instructors can show you how to, uh, restrain someone," he explained, "the agents at the non-field training headquarters teach you *who* to restrain and *why.*"

Fenwick pulled Nicki's luggage from the carousel, then

searched for his own. Heathrow Airport was at its busiest during the summer, with tourists flying in and out of London by the thousands.

At sixteen, Nicki Haddon had been in more international airports than most people ever visited in a lifetime, and Heathrow was one of the ones she frequented most often. But this arrival was different. This was the first time she was traveling anywhere as a newly recruited spy-in-training. She spent the almost eight-hour flight from Toronto wrapping her head around the idea. She hadn't hesitated to accept the invitation, but she knew she couldn't fully anticipate what lay ahead. But then, her kung fu training prepared her to be open to all eventualities.

"You still haven't told me where this place is," said Nicki. She and Fenwick hadn't been able to talk openly on their flight from Toronto.

"In an old sugar factory on Adder Street. In the East End, near the docks." He raised an eyebrow. "So it's a good thing indeed that you're an expert in kung fu."

"Tough neighborhood?" Nicki's numerous London visits had always been centered in the downtown core.

"The worst," he replied. "You'll see when you go to Adder Street for classes tomorrow morning."

"Do I need a key?"

"No, Miss. Your iris will be scanned, and the computers will be set to allow you access."

"So did you go to this school?" asked Nicki.

"No, I didn't. I was sent to a location in Hampshire, but

that was after I had finished training as a butler. And after I'd spent quite a few years in the Royal Air Force."

"I didn't know you were a pilot."

"Oh, yes," replied the gray-haired butler. "Helicopters and small aircraft."

"But you told me you grew up in the East End." She watched as a group of teenagers dashed past, laughing as they ran to catch their flight.

"Yes, my sister Emma and I grew up there. Penniless." He checked his watch. "Which is why I eventually took a position at MI6."

"And then you moved to Milchester?"

"No, I only recently bought the cottage. I bought it for—" He stopped himself, leaving Nicki to wonder why. She didn't pry, and he carried on. "Emma is expecting us there in a few hours."

"By the way, I've been meaning to ask—how did you arrange a leave of absence with my parents?" While attempting to recruit Nicki for the British spy agency, Fenwick had been working undercover as a butler at the Haddons' home on Toronto's exclusive Bridle Path. The Haddons owned an upscale chain of hotels around the world and had adopted Nicki from China as an infant. Once agents for the Canadian Security Intelligence Service and the United States Secret Service saw Nicki in action, they also wanted her aboard. Carrying dual citizenship and being a kung fu champion, Nicki was considered a natural for international intelligence work.

"Since your parents believe that you're here to train at a

martial arts school for elite athletes," explained the butler, "I suggested accompanying you to London to look after your needs and help get you settled. They weren't going to be needing me much, what with all their upcoming travel, so they agreed." He spotted his suitcase on the belt. "Oh, there it is," he said. Just as he grabbed his bag, his cell phone rang.

Nicki surveyed the airport. Crowds of people brushed by her. Every time she landed in England, it struck her as a country of extremes. On the one hand, London was a bustling, energetic, overwhelming, impersonal metropolis where no one had a minute for anyone else. Yet within that very city stood eternal cathedrals and palaces, unaffected by the ravages of time. Their leaded windows were like looking-glasses into the far and misty past.

"Today?" asked Fenwick into his phone. "But I—" He listened intently. "I see," he said. "Yes, immediately." He returned the phone to a pocket inside his jacket.

"What's that all about?" asked Nicki, moving aside to let a flower seller squeeze her cart past.

Fenwick lowered his voice. "I'm sorry, Miss Nicki, but it looks as if I won't be accompanying you to Milchester after all." He pulled his luggage toward him and waited while two groups of women filed by. "Things are moving along a bit faster than I expected."

"What do you mean?" asked Nicki.

"I had hoped to fill you in on the way to my sister's, but as it turns out, they want you to go there alone." The flower seller pushed past a second time, so Nicki and the butler moved. He checked the location of the overhead surveillance cameras, then chose a spot behind a pillar to disclose the information. "As for me, I will be working out of Buckingham," he said softly.

"Buckingham *Palace?*" whispered Nicki. "As a butler?"

"Yes, Miss." He noticed a tourist snapping photos of the airport and instinctively turned his head. "A few days ago, there was a security breach at the palace. Someone made it past the guards, in the dead of night. I'm told he got as far as the library before escaping on foot."

"Did the cameras at the palace pick up an image of the intruder?"

"A young man, but he was wearing a hood."

"Did he take anything?"

"It appears the intruder didn't find what he was looking for," replied Fenwick. "But a security breach of that magnitude can mean only one thing, of course."

"This person had help. Someone let him in."

Fenwick nodded. "They've arrested one of the guards. I'm sure he was paid off handsomely."

"Right," agreed Nicki. "He'll never talk."

In addition to her kung fu talent, it was also this instinctive insight into criminal activity that had singled Nicki out as a strong candidate for intelligence work. It didn't hurt that she was a big fan of James Bond movies and had read all fourteen of Ian Fleming's Bond books. Fenwick had to remind himself that she was a complete neophyte, having just been recruited.

"We have reason to believe the intruder was part of a syndicate of drug smugglers. You've been tagged as being well suited to assist with our efforts to help crack the syndicate. There is a young man staying at my sister's house—the son of one of her friends. I don't know his connection to the drug cartel, but—"

"And that's why you're having me stay there? To watch him?"

Fenwick gave a wry smile. "You will soon learn that in this business, Miss Nicki, there are always two sides to everything. Your training starts first thing tomorrow. Once you find the old sugar factory on Adder Street, look for a large ventilation shaft at street level. Behind that shaft, you will see black fire escape doors that appear to open only from the inside. Enter through those doors, take the steps down, and follow the tunnel underground." He looked at his watch. "I really have to get to the palace."

"Can you handle it?" Nicki asked. "I mean, serving the royals?"

"I've buttled for the best," he replied.

"Buttled?"

"Yes, Miss. It *is* a verb, you know."

Nicki smiled. "Will you be the only MI6 operative at the palace?" she asked.

"No. I'll have backup."

"How do I contact you?"

Fenwick pulled a cell phone from his luggage. "You will use this phone, and only this phone, if you need to reach me. It can't be traced to you. See that no one has access to it, because if a text comes to me from this device, I will assume that it is from you."

"What about my other phone?"

Fenwick held out his hand.

"Turn it over?" asked Nicki, and the butler nodded.

"Your new phone has...well, let's just say it has advantages."

"Advantages?"

"It can self-destruct instantly, should the need arise."

"Self de—? You're kidding me," said Nicki.

"It looks like any other cell phone, but it is sealed with epoxy and has screws that, if tampered with, will trigger an immediate reaction so that the phone will delete both the software and the data contained within. Now, if someone attempts to take it from your person, and you want everything deleted immediately—for instance if a call is in progress—simply push this." He slid back a small panel on the bottom of the phone and pointed to a red button hidden beneath it.

"Got it," said Nicki, "although I like my old phone better." She smiled. "It's got all my photos on it, including pictures of my parents at our home in Hawaii."

She was referring to the Haddons, of course, but whenever Nicki used the word "parents" she thought of four people—the Haddons and the couple in China who had abandoned her at birth. She touched the charm that hung around her neck, the one that had been found with her on the roadside in China. *They must have cared about me. Why else would they leave me with a good luck charm?*

"I'll keep your phone somewhere safe," promised Fenwick. "But in the meantime, this will be your only phone. It's untraceable outside intelligence circles, but for those inside we've taken the liberty of listing it under your alias, Fu Yin. Use it when you talk to anyone at MI6. Use it when you talk to anyone at the FBI. And Miss?"

"Yes?"

"We'll be managing your social media accounts for the time being."

"Oh, no!" declared Nicki. "I was hoping to keep in touch with my friends in Toronto. Find out what they're doing, anyway."

"We can't run the risk of anyone tracing you. Your friends Margo and T'ai won't have their suspicions raised—as far as they'll know, you'll be at martial arts school in London—but you won't be able to contact them yourself for the foreseeable future." Nicki had only just met Margo Bloom and T'ai Soong in Toronto, but Margo had become a treasured friend and T'ai an almost boyfriend. "You must remember, Miss, that while it's true the secret service taps into Facebook and Instagram and the like all the time, so too do the foreign operatives."

"Okay," Nicki replied. "I get it."

"And if you have to call your parents," he added, "it would be best to make a collect call from a pay phone."

"Hey, I remember pay phones," she said with a straight face. "They run on steam, right?"

"Very funny, Miss Nicki," said Fenwick.

"So," said Nicki, "does this mean that no one at the school knows who I am?"

"Only those at the very top levels of the SIS, the CIA, and of course the Canadian Security Intelligence Service know that you are Nicki Haddon. It is simply too risky otherwise. You cannot trust anyone in this business." The butler looked around the other side of the pillar. "Another agent could be working for Russia or China, or even for the mob."

"What about Grand Master Kahana?" asked Nicki, referring to the kung fu master who had helped recruit her as a spy. "How do I communicate with him?"

"When he feels it's necessary, he will contact you from a secure mobile that can't be tapped. Because of his work with the CIA, his conversations are monitored frequently." The butler smiled. "He'll be out of the hospital soon."

"I hope so."

"And I know he's very proud of how you handled the whole Ming vase affair for him." Fenwick picked up his luggage. "Now remember, Miss, my sister has no knowledge of my work in the secret service."

"What do I tell her? That you're working for the royal family?"

"No. Tell Emma I took a position somewhere in Westminster. You don't know exactly where."

"What about me? What do I tell her about myself?"

"That you are Fu Yin. That you are studying kung fu in the city's East End. That I am a friend of your parents and that you needed a place to stay in England." The butler turned to leave. "She needs...she needs the money, Miss Nicki. She's quite happy that I found a boarder for her." He walked away.

"I'll see you," said Nicki, but Fenwick did not turn around and did not reply in kind.

Nicki looked up to the overhead sign to find her way to the bus depot. Although she'd been to London many times, her parents always had a limo waiting to sweep her off to the luxurious Haddon Gardens Hotel in South Kensington. Taking the discount coach to Milchester was altogether new.

She purchased her ticket, then noticed the bus wouldn't be leaving until later that evening.

"Is there nothing sooner?" she asked the clerk.

"You just missed it. Sorry."

Next to the wicket was a large map of the different routes out of London. While she studied it, she sensed that someone was watching her from behind a newspaper stand.

The flower seller. Why is she staring at me?

Turning her head just slightly, Nicki watched out of the corner of her eye as the woman pulled out a cell phone and held it in the air.

She's taking my picture!

The woman started texting.

And now she's sending it to someone.

The flower seller shoved the phone into a pocket on her apron and swung her cart back into the crowd. Nicki followed, and before long, several people had circled around the cart to buy bouquets.

Nicki scrutinized the vendor carefully. Her dress was faded and her red hair somewhat disheveled. Oddly, however, her shoes were brand new. And they were not cheap by any means. Nicki recognized the Gucci flats instantly because her mother had a similar pair.

How can a flower seller afford six hundred dollar shoes?

The woman spotted Nicki in line and hurried her customers through. Nicki moved forward and jammed her foot in front of the wheel of the cart.

"Oh, these bouquets are lovely," said Nicki.

"Yes," the woman said curtly, her head down.

"I like this one," Nicki said. "What are those dried stems?" She pointed to some globe-shaped seed pods arranged with spikes of purple blooms and tied with a green and white vine.

"Poppy seed pods," mumbled the woman, keeping her head lowered. "Miss, I'm in a bit of a rush." She tried to push away, but Nicki's foot prevented the cart from rolling.

"I love this bouquet, but it's quite expensive."

"The pods are imported."

"Imported? From where?" asked Nicki.

"From, uh, the Middle East. Look, I have to go..."

"The purple flowers—they're foxgloves?" Nicki asked, and the woman nodded. "They're beautiful, but they're deadly poison, aren't they? Is it safe to handle them?" Nicki remembered the family's gardener in Hawaii calling them Dead Men's Bells.

"Here, take this one instead." The woman held out a smaller bouquet that had the poppy pods arranged with lilies and carnations.

"Perfect. I'll take it." Nicki left the vendor holding the bouquet while she pulled some cash from her shoulder bag and handed it to her. While the woman set down the bouquet and rummaged in her pocket for change, Nicki slipped out her phone. "Everything is so lovely, I think I'll snap a photo." *And make sure that you're in it.*

The woman threw her arm up to cover her face, but Nicki already had what she wanted. She grabbed the flowers and took off, melting into the crowd.

Chapter Two

The bus trip through the suburbs of London wouldn't have been too bad if it hadn't been for the guy breathing down her neck. Nicki figured he was two or three years older than herself, but his bloodshot eyes and haggard expression made him look older than that.

What's his problem? she wondered.

He'd boarded the bus with her at Heathrow and had pushed through the line to get the seat directly behind her. Although she'd never seen him before, Nicki sensed that he was following her.

When he got off behind her at Milchester, she knew she was right.

Could he be the young man who's staying with Emma?

The sun was beginning to set, and most of the town's

residents were either relaxing at home or having a pint at the local pub. Nicki spotted a man on the opposite side of the street, walking his spaniel. She crossed the road to ask him for directions. When she did, her guy from the bus stopped and lit a cigarette.

"About ten doors down on your right," said the dog walker. He made a face. "It's the place with the weeds."

"Thanks," said Nicki.

"And the noise," added the man.

"Noise?"

"You'll find out."

Nicki wheeled her luggage down the empty winding street that led to Emma's cottage, watching as the bus guy shadowed her from the other side. Several doors away from Emma's, she tossed the bouquet onto the grass, let go of her suitcase, and bolted across the road toward him. The guy jumped over a hedge, ran down a ravine, and disappeared into the darkness.

Coward, she thought.

She wanted to go after him but couldn't leave her suitcase sitting on the street, so she headed for Emma's, making sure he was nowhere in sight.

As she approached the small stone cottage, Nicki heard blaring music; it was coming from a shed out back. She didn't know the song and could make out only some of the lyrics:

> *"Come out of the cupboard, you boys and girls*
> *London calling, now don't look to us*
> *Phoney Beatlemania has bitten the dust."*

That music is live, thought Nicki. She lifted the garden gate over a clump of thistles and pushed through to the backyard. There wasn't much point in knocking, so she let herself in.

Three women, all in their forties, thrashed out the song under a banner that said, "The Leather Daisies." With their iridescently streaked hair shaved halfway up the sides of their heads, their deliberately shredded clothes, and heavy leather boots, it was clear they were punk rockers.

Standing against the wall, listening, was a young man, about eighteen years old. *There he is. The guy Fenwick wants me to keep an eye on.* Nicki decided she was going to like this first assignment. With his dark hair and eyes, he had a look she found very attractive.

"London calling, see we ain't got no swing
'Cept for the ring of that truncheon thing."

The woman on bass was clearly East Indian and the drummer was black, so Nicki knew right away that the lead guitarist was Fenwick's sister, despite the pink hair and numerous piercings in her left eyebrow.

Once the women spotted her, the music stopped.

"Who are you?" asked Emma, her voice as cold as the ice in the cooler next to her feet.

"Fu Yin."

"*You're* my new boarder?" She had a thick cockney accent.

"Yes."

Emma turned to the drummer. "My brother's idea of

therapy, I guess." She started adjusting her guitar strings, ignoring Nicki completely.

Therapy? wondered Nicki. She handed the flowers to Emma, who tossed them on the floor without a word. She set her guitar between two beat-up amplifiers, found an empty plastic jug, used it to scoop some melted ice water out of the cooler, then jammed in the flowers.

"Poppy seed pods," she muttered. Her cockney accent was so different from Fenwick's upper-crust Etonian intonation, Nicki couldn't believe they had grown up together in the same part of London.

As if to make up for Emma's rudeness, the young man came over and handed Nicki a can of pop from the cooler.

Nicki felt strange when his eyes met hers. He was not handsome in the traditional sense, but the attraction was undeniable. And the way he stared at her, she wondered for a second if he felt the same. Slightly unnerved, she turned away and looked up at the banner hanging over the band.

The young man followed her gaze. "The Leather Daisies. Get it?"

Nicki shook her head.

"Daisies are boots in cockney slang," he explained. "You know, daisy roots—hard to pull up. Like boots."

Emma interrupted. "I'm guessing by the flowers and the look on your face that you were expecting something else here. What's the matter? Don't you like The Clash?"

"Sure she likes them," said the young man. "Don't you, Fu Yin?" He gave her a long look—so long and intense, Nicki had to turn away again. He coughed, and Nicki thought it odd that he would have a cold at this time of year. "Do we call you Yin?"

She nodded. "And you are...?"

"Sid," he replied. "Mother named me after Sid Vicious." He put an arm around the bass player and smiled. "Could've been worse. She could have called me Johnny Rotten."

"Vicious?" Nicki asked.

"You know—from The Sex Pistols."

"Oh, right," she replied. Nicki didn't know much punk rock.

Emma was not impressed. "Look, if you don't like it here..." She left the sentence hanging, and Sid jumped to Nicki's defense.

"Cut the girl some slack, will you, Emma?" he said.

"It isn't that I don't like it here," said Nicki. "It's just that Fenwick didn't mention—"

"Who's Fenwick?"

Now I've done it, thought Nicki.

"I mean, your brother, the butler, Mr. Wright."

"Why'd you call him Fenwick?"

"Uh...where he worked in Toronto, they called him Fenwick. I don't know why."

"Oh," said Emma. "Where is he anyway?"

"He said to tell you that he's taken a position in Westminster."

"Must be nice," said the drummer, standing up to stretch. "So you're a Canuck. What are you doing here in Jolly Ol'?"

"I'm here to study kung fu," replied Nicki.

"Kung fu? You're kidding me," said Emma.

Being slight of build and just five foot two, Nicki was used to people's incredulity. She didn't respond.

"C'mon, Emma," said Sid. "If she wants to try and learn martial arts, it's up to her."

"You can't blame me for being surprised," said Emma. "She's so...I don't know...fragile-looking."

The drummer changed the subject. "I'm Dawn Chebet, by the way," she said. "And that's Anika Jabbar." She pointed to the bass player. "Anika and Sid are staying here in Milchester with Emma for a while."

"We're only here until I'm back on my feet," said Anika. "I'm out of work right now." She looked at Nicki. "So you're... Chinese?"

Nicki nodded. "And you're..."

"Bangladeshi."

"And I'm Kenyan," said Dawn. "Anika, Emma, and I grew up together," she explained. "And Sid is our sound man."

"So you're in high school, Yin?" asked Sid.

"No, I finished early. But I won't be going to college—not for a few years, anyway. I want to focus on my martial arts training."

Nicki had been tutored in Hawaii. She had the marks to go to the university of her choice but had decided, even before being recruited as a spy, to concentrate on kung fu and continue to compete on an international level.

Emma picked up her guitar and played a riff. "I wish you'd move in here, Dawn. Then I wouldn't need to take in a—" She stopped.

A boarder. Like me. Right, thought Nicki.

"All of us? Living under the same roof?" said Anika. "Get real." She laughed.

Emma must have decided she needed to at least try to be nice to her new boarder. Keeping her eyes fixed on her guitar, she asked Nicki, "So how'd you meet Willie anyway?"

"Willie?"

"My brother. How'd you meet him?"

"Oh, he's a friend of my parents." Nicki looked away and saw a face peering into the window of the shed.

That's the guy from the bus!

Chapter Three

Nicki bolted out the door.

"Hey, what's up?" called Sid, following her into the yard. Dawn, Anika, and Emma were right behind him.

The bus guy tried to run away, but Nicki wasn't about to let him escape this time. Gaining on him quickly, she propelled herself forward and threw her feet into the air. The forward jump kick made him lose his balance and he fell face down. He struggled to get up again, but Nicki was an international champion in the art of wushu and had trained in kung fu dim mak pressure points. She pushed her toe into the base of his neck and immobilized him instantly.

She applied more force until he held up his hand to stop her. "Okay, okay," he sputtered.

Sid turned to Anika and Dawn. "She must be a fast learner," he said with a grin.

"Should we call the cops?" Anika asked Emma.

"I wouldn't do that—" The stalker winced when Nicki moved her foot to the center of his back.

"Todd?" said Sid. "Get up, will you?" Sid grabbed the back of the guy's shirt and gave it a yank. Then he turned to Nicki. "Wow. You're good. You've been at this a while, haven't you?"

Nicki gave a little nod. "So you know this guy," she said. "Then why was he peering through the window?"

The Peeping Tom gave her an angry look, then brushed off his legs and the front of his shirt.

"Yeah, we know him, all right," said Anika. "His name's Todd Bead, and he's been a friend of Sid's since grade school. Haven't seen him around for a while, though, ever since he got mixed up with the Belden Street Gang."

"What are you doing, spying on us through the window?" asked Emma.

"Yeah, what's up with that, Todd?" Sid asked with a smile. "You're gonna have to watch yourself around here now that we've got a black belt living with us."

"What's she doing hanging around a cop?" blurted Bead.

"What cop?" asked Sid.

"She was with a guy at the airport," insisted Bead. "He's some kind of a cop or—"

"Cop!" Emma practically choked on the word. "That was my brother, you clod!"

Bead looked at Nicki.

"That's right," she said, grateful for the cover that Emma had unknowingly provided.

"Smarten up, Bead," snapped Emma. "No more peering through windows, okay?" She headed back to the shed, and her bandmates followed her inside.

"What's going on, mate?" Sid asked Bead. He took hold of his friend's arm and turned it over to look at the inside. Todd snatched it back, but not before Nicki saw the telltale tracks of heroin use.

"You need to get over to the meth clinic. You really do," said Sid. "I'll go with you, if you want." Sid started coughing again. He pulled out a lozenge and stuck it in his mouth.

"I came here to warn you," said Bead.

"Warn me?"

Bead didn't answer his friend, but scowled at Nicki instead.

"I'm not leaving," Nicki said. "And you know why." *If he hadn't been secretly following me, he wouldn't have peered through the window. He would have knocked at the door.*

"Why?" asked Sid, but Nicki just kept her gaze on Bead.

Bead ignored her and turned to his friend. "The cops. They're coming to ask you questions. I didn't do it, Sid, really I didn't. You've gotta believe me."

"What are you talking about?"

Bead headed out to the street, walking so fast he was almost running. "They'll be here soon, mate."

"Todd?" hollered Sid, but the guy kept walking. He pulled out a cell phone and started scrolling through it.

Nicki started after him. "I want to speak with you for a minute," she called to him.

"I got nothing to say," he replied, still moving at a clip. But when Nicki caught up to him, he stopped; he wasn't looking to get pinned down a second time. "What is it?" he snapped. He kept his eyes on his phone. He was fumbling with it, shielding it from Nicki's view.

"Why'd you follow me from the airport?"

He didn't answer, just kept fiddling with his phone. Nicki snatched it from him and saw her photo staring back at her.

That's the photo the flower seller snapped at the airport! She must have sent it to him.

Todd tried to grab his phone back, but Nicki was expert in evading aggressors. As she kept him at bay, she checked for the sender's ID, but it had been removed. She deleted her photo, then opened the next one. It was of a dull-looking middle-aged man, purchasing pills from a pharmacist.

"Give me my phone!" demanded Bead. By this point, Sid had caught up to them. He was coughing, unable to move very fast.

"Not before you tell me who that flower seller is and why she had you follow me," said Nicki, jamming the cell into her pocket.

"What?" Sid turned to his friend. "What's she talking about?" He looked at Nicki. "Flower seller?"

Bead threw his hands in the air. "I can't stand it. I can't stand this life."

"Todd," said Sid. "I want to help you. You said if I got

that money out for you, you would rent a place. Get a job. Go straight."

"What do you mean, 'got money out' for him?" asked Nicki, steering clear of questions about the flower seller.

Bead broke in. "They linked the bank card with the footage from the surveillance camera, mate. That's why they're coming for you. Get out of town, Sid. Get out of town."

"I did nothing wrong," Sid said. "I'm not going anywhere."

"You're stupid, really," said Bead, walking away. "I'm outta here."

And you forgot your phone, thought Nicki.

She turned to Sid. "I don't think he's kidding around," she said, but she could tell by the look on Sid's face that he knew that already. He didn't say a word. "Okay, if you're not going to tell me about the money, maybe you'll tell me where Bead lives?" she asked. *That way I can go and ask him myself.*

"Wherever he can find a place to sleep," said Sid. He was saying the words, but his mind was someplace else. "Usually on the bench in front of the methadone clinic in the East End."

"Well, that's good, anyway."

"No it isn't," he replied. "Everyone knows the meth clinic is the best place to buy drugs."

Chapter Four

When Nicki arrived at the training facility on Adder Street the next morning, a technician took her fingerprints and recorded her voice.

"This voice recognition software," he said, "is accurate to within one hundred million. So if you are in the field and are in trouble, our computers will know instantly if it is you calling or if it is an impostor."

"What if someone forces me to call and give false information?"

"The computer will analyze your tone and breathing pattern and alert the command center if you are in distress. And as a backup, your code word under those circumstances is 'butterfly.' Commit it to memory. If you are not in danger, the word to use is…" He punched some keys on his computer. "The word to indicate that you are safe is 'spruce.'"

"Got it," said Nicki.

The technician handed her an ID card in the name of Fu Yin. "This will identify you to the other assets."

"Assets?"

"Agents," he explained. "Now, stand here and look into the window." He gestured to the biometric locking mechanism, a circular piece of heavy steel set into the doorframe, with a window made from tempered blue glass. Nicki had trouble reaching at first but managed to stretch high enough by standing on the tips of her toes. A series of beeps meant that her iris had been scanned.

"Good," said the technician. "All set. You enter the training area through there."

Nicki stood in front of two thick steel doors. A line of red lights blinked, the doors parted, and Nicki walked through. The doors thundered shut behind her. A sign on the wall advised her to shut off any electronic devices, so she turned off her cell phone.

She passed through three more sets of security gates. What awaited her was a rather unremarkable classroom. A heavyset, sweaty man stood at the front; his rumpled clothing made him look like a large unmade bed.

"7347?" he asked.

I know him. He's the man whose photo is on Todd Bead's cell phone. She wondered if she should mention it to him, then remembered that Fenwick told her not to trust anyone, even other "assets."

"7347?" he repeated. His eyes were small and angry.

Nicki checked the card the technician had given her. It said nothing of the British Secret Intelligence Service, nor CSIS. In fact, although it incorporated the most up-to-date chip technology and probably had every possible security feature available, it was made to look like a student card for an institute of cosmetology and esthetics.

Cosmetology? Give me a break.

"7347?"

"Yes," she replied.

"Repeat the number for me."

"7347."

"Take a seat."

She was at least ten to twenty years younger than the other student spies; every eye was on her as she found a desk near the wall.

"My name is Warren Letch," said the instructor. He spoke through his teeth, barely moving his lips. "Inside this facility, you will refer to me as Mr. Letch. I will be using your numerical code to address you. And that is how you will address each other during class. On lunch, or at break time, you may use each other's street names."

A hand went up.

"What?" said Letch.

"What about outside the facility?" asked a man in the back row.

Letch rolled his eyes. "Outside these walls you do not

address each other at all. Outside these walls you don't know each other. You've never heard of each other. You don't know that each other exists. Do I make myself clear?"

The man nodded.

Letch began the class with a demonstration of some of the software used by the intelligence agents. He flashed a series of faces onto a giant touch screen at the front of the room. Next to each face was more biographical information than the person probably knew about himself. Besides the usual things like date of birth and any known aliases, the information included every place that person had ever been, every friend they'd ever had, every Internet site they'd visited. And, just as Fenwick had said, every entry on their social media accounts and a list of every time they'd accessed someone else's.

When Letch touched one of the faces, a map appeared on the left of the screen showing where the person had last been seen. Another touch and the most recent surveillance camera footage played, zooming in with such detail that Nicki could read the ticket stub in one man's hand. It was for a lecture at the Natural History Museum. The caption underneath read, "Xavier Zidane, Top Ten Most Wanted List."

Letch started barking out information. "The days of waiting for a warrant to do an overt search of someone's mail are over," he said. "We have the equipment to monitor the conversations of terrorists, the text messages of assassins, and the e-mails between members of organized crime." He displayed some examples. "The problem is that they know we do. So they have started using codes in some of their communications.

Sometimes these codes are so advanced, we need specially trained agents to break them."

A hand went up. "So does that mean that some codes are not always so difficult to decipher?" asked an older woman in the front row.

"When members of a crime syndicate need to relay information quickly—for example, to gang members who are working for them—they may resort to a simpler code, something these guys on the street can deal with."

"Not for highly classified information," the woman remarked.

"Right. It would be to relay directions, something like that," said Letch. He slugged back water from a dirty-looking glass.

"At this stage in your training as intelligence officers," he continued, "you will learn kinesic lie detection, so you can tell by the way a guy scratches his head whether or not he's telling the truth. This goes for those of you who have been recruited for domestic security with MI5 as well as those who will be initiating offensive operations in other countries as MI6 officers. A few of you...," he glanced at Nicki, and it wasn't a friendly glance, "a few of you are here for special operations." He returned to the big screen and started pulling up faces again.

"The individuals you see before you," said Letch, "are currently planning one of the most hideous attacks on western civilization." He touched each one until the enlarged photo filled the entire frame. "And not one of these individuals is a terrorist. Not one is a suicide bomber. These men are not radicals or extremists." He put down his pointer, then cracked his knuckles for punctuation. "So, you are asking, how are these people going to destroy not only Britain, but the entire developed world?"

He touched the screen again.

"With this pretty little flower." He moved back so everyone could take a good look.

It was an opium poppy.

"Open your boxes," said Letch. He folded his arms. "Go on. They won't bite you."

"What is this?" asked one of the students, holding up a tiny piece of metal, no bigger than a pin.

"That is an identification transmitter. The smallest and most precise available today. Hidden inside your shoe, it enables our satellites to determine your exact geographical location." He gave a wry smile. "In case we need to find you."

Then his expression changed. "In time, of course, you will require a subcutaneous implant. This will have to do for now."

Nicki peeled off the foil backing and placed the device securely inside the tongue of her left shoe. *This is a good place for it—I'm never out of these running shoes.*

Letch picked up his pointer and dimmed the lights. "Let's take one more look at these faces," he said.

"These men are members of the largest heroin cartel on the face of the planet. We've just recently identified Xavier Zidane as their ringleader here in the UK. We're gathering what intelligence we can, but the guy is very evasive. We know next to nothing about his personal life.

"Organized crime controls the production, importation, and sale of illicit drugs," Letch continued. "The higher the strength of the opiates they can get from the East, the higher the rate of addiction they can generate. Which is exactly what these creeps want, right? The more addicts, the more money." He pushed the back of his shirt into his pants where it had come untucked. "It's like mass murder committed over time."

Students were nodding their heads in agreement.

"When it comes to guys like this, we have a motto here in the secret service," continued Letch. "Follow the money. Remember that."

"Money laundering?" asked one of the students.

"By the time you are finished here, you will know every kind of laundering scheme available." He wiped his forehead with a tissue, then carried on. "Right now, we know that somebody in this country is managing to send a lot of money to illegal poppy growers in Turkey and Afghanistan. And is getting away with it."

Nicki focused on the screen behind Letch. Faces, names, maps—with each click, they swept by like a high-tech rogues' gallery. Returning to the shot of Xavier Zidane, Letch pulled up photographs of the man's recent contacts. One of them caught her eye. It was a fuzzy shot, taken of a young man withdrawing cash from an automatic teller. Beneath the picture, the screen said:

Sid Jabbar
Member, Belden Street Gang
Incarcerated but uncooperative
Limehouse Prison

Incarcerated! They must have just picked him up this morning. But he's not a member of the gang—is he?

★ ★ ★

"I know you'll keep your wits about you at all times, Nicki. We don't want you falling into any traps." The caller was David Kahana, one of the world's most distinguished experts in kung fu. He was also an American spy who had recently been stabbed while transporting a precious Ming vase. He was calling from Toronto to let Nicki know that he was finally being released from hospital.

Kahana stopped talking for a minute while someone shuffled in and out of his hospital room. Nicki, who was waiting for the bus back to Milchester, heard the clatter of a tray, then the sound of a door closing.

Kahana continued. "Both Scotland Yard and the Secret Intelligence Service admit to having disreputable members in their ranks. The temptation to take a payoff is omnipresent, and even some of our best agents have been bought out eventually. You can't trust anyone, Nicki. No one. These people are making millions—billions, even—so they wouldn't hesitate to kill whoever gets in their way."

Nicki turned around to be sure no one was behind her, listening to her conversation. "Does the FBI have any doubts about Warren Letch? I'd like to know why a gang member has his photo on his phone."

"Could be the gang has discovered Letch is an agent and wanted to warn their members to steer clear of him. I'll let MI6 know that Letch may be at risk. Meanwhile, your age is your best cover and our best chance for infiltrating the syndicate. It's the young people on the front lines who are doing the dirty work for the cartel."

"And paying the price," added Nicki, thinking of Todd and Sid. She spotted her bus several blocks away. "I've got to go soon, but I want to tell you how happy I am that you're being made a Supreme Grand Master. It's wonderful." She sighed. "I wish I could be in Shanghai this weekend to see you receive the title."

"I wish you could, too. But you're where you need to be."

Nicki chose her next words carefully. "Master Kahana?"

"Yes?"

"I don't want to put any extra work on you right now, but since you are going to be in China, I was wondering—"

"I've got that covered, Nicki," he replied. "I promised you that I would help find your birth parents, and I will. I am going to the orphanage myself, and I—"

"Thank you, Master Kahana. It means everything to me. I'm sorry—my bus. I have to go."

She ended the call just as the bus pulled up to her stop and the doors opened for her. She hesitated.

"Gettin' on?" hollered the driver.

"Uh, no, I guess not," said Nicki. The doors started to close. "Wait!" she yelled. "Can you tell me which bus goes to Limehouse Prison?"

★　★　★

Nicki looked up at the burly female prison guard who towered over her. "May I have permission to visit one of the inmates? His name is Sid Jabbar. I realize that I'm only—"

"Fourteen. I'm guessing fourteen."

"Sixteen."

"I would have said fourteen."

"Can I visit my, uh, friend?"

"No."

"No? That's it?" asked Nicki.

"Not unless an adult family member gets you a pass." The guard stopped to check someone's identification, then let him through the heavy door.

"Can you make an exception for me this once?"

"No."

Nicki turned to leave, but the guard stopped her.

"Look, you seem like a nice kid. Jabbar's mother is in there with him now. If she agrees to it, I can let you speak to him."

"Great," said Nicki. She waited patiently, and before long she was cleared for admittance and was led to Sid and his mother.

"How are you, Sid?" asked Nicki.

"I've been better."

"Yin," Anika said, her eyes filled with tears. "Thanks for coming. But how did you hear about Sid's arrest?" asked Anika. "The police came after you left."

"Uh…" Nicki couldn't tell them she'd just found out from the secret service.

"Todd told her last night that they were after me," said Sid. He was clearly exhausted, and Nicki figured he'd been questioned for hours. His face was unshaven, his hair unkempt, but she still found him attractive.

Then he coughed. And it wasn't a dry little cough—it was the long, hacking, choking kind.

Anika let her head drop to her chest.

"It's okay, Mom," said Sid. "I'm all right. Look, I don't want you to be worrying, okay?"

"It's too late for that. Once you got involved with those people—whoever they are—well, that was it right there. Now look where you are." Anika tried to control her emotions but couldn't; she left to clean up her face.

"Sid, who are 'those people'?" asked Nicki. "Are they the ones who gave Todd the bank card?"

"Even if I knew, I wouldn't tell you, because you'd be shot within twenty-four hours," he said.

"Look, I figure Todd was being paid to do something for someone with lots of money. I heard something on the news about a break-in at Buckingham Palace. Police have said they think it was a young man, an inexperienced thief, likely someone with a drug addiction. I couldn't help wondering whether

Todd might be the one who did it. Maybe that's what he was paid to do. But why? What was it they wanted him to take?"

"Please stay out of it, okay? Why are you so interested in Todd? What could you do anyway?"

Anika returned and Sid stood up. He pressed his hand against the Plexiglas that separated him from his mother. She did the same, and the prison guards hustled him back to his cell. Anika collapsed into her chair.

Nicki turned to her. "I know you're worried about his cold, but there must be a nurse here who can help him."

"Maybe, but Yin, Sid's cough is much worse than just a cold," said Anika. "I'm terrified he'll…"

"Terrified he'll what?"

Anika looked Nicki straight in the eyes.

"I can't lose him. He's all I've got."

Chapter Five

"I'm sorry to hear about the young man, Miss Nicki," said Fenwick. "Believe me, I understand what poverty can do to people. How desperate it can make them."

Nicki whispered into her cell phone. "I really don't think Sid had anything to do with the break-in at the palace. He withdrew the cash, but it was for his friend—Todd Bead." Nicki had called the butler once she was back in her room at Emma's cottage. "They've set the bail so high, Anika doesn't have a hope of getting Sid out of there. My parents could lend me the money. I could tell them it's my fee for the academy, something like that..." She drew a deep breath.

"I think the young man on the palace security cameras might have been Bead," she continued. "I tried to get Sid to tell me, but he wouldn't. I think Sid's a good guy. I really do."

"I agree with you. I've known the boy for years. But he could know more than he's telling you." Fenwick didn't mince words. "We are certain that the syndicate is behind this. These are not ordinary criminals we're dealing with, Miss Nicki. These are the cream of the crop, so to speak, and they don't like any loose ends. Sid Jabbar is, unfortunately, exactly that. He's much safer in prison than out."

Nicki sighed. "I guess you're right. But he's just a pawn. Surely there's something we can do to help him and his mom."

"We can't get sidetracked. There's too much at stake," said the butler. "GCHQ has deciphered a series of messages, and from what they tell me, the situation is grave."

"GCHQ?" asked Nicki. "Mr. Letch hasn't mentioned that one yet."

"He will," replied Fenwick. "Government Communications Headquarters, GCHQ, consists of supercomputers that eavesdrop on phone calls, e-mails, text messages—you name it—and decoding experts who decipher the results."

"What have they picked up?"

"We haven't got all the details yet, but it appears that one of the largest opium exporters in Turkey, a fellow by the name of Osman, is going to be in London within the next week for some type of exchange. And from what my superiors tell me, if this does happen—well, it won't be good."

"Did the SIS tell you anything else?"

"They don't know anything else. And even if they do, it may be in their best interest to keep it quiet for a while. It's like I told you before, Miss Nicki, everything is strictly on a need-to-know basis. Too many things could go wrong."

"That's why I haven't told Warren Letch about his photograph appearing on Bead's phone."

"What do you mean?"

"I'm sure that Sid is being linked to the Belden Street Gang because of his friend, Todd Bead. Bead followed me from Heathrow to Emma's place, and when I grabbed his phone, I found a picture of myself taken by that flower seller at the airport. And Mr. Letch's photo was there as well. Bead took off so quickly, he forgot his phone. I wonder if you could have Bead's cell bugged by your friends over there at GCHQ."

"Probably. What are you thinking?"

"It might lead somewhere. The SIS has connected Sid with someone named Zidane, probably because of Bead—"

"Yes, Miss Nicki. Xavier Zidane, the head of the syndicate here in the UK." Fenwick paused, and she could hear voices around him. "I have to serve evening tea to a group of dignitaries in another minute. Don't attempt to bring Bead's phone here. I will come out to Emma's tomorrow morning," he said. "By the way, are you comfortable there?"

"Sure. I don't need much more than a bed and a closet."

"Oh—she put you up in that tiny spare room, did she?"

"Well," replied Nicki, "I guess Anika's staying in the second bedroom. And Sid's been sleeping out in the shed."

"Right," said the butler. "As long as you're fine with it."

"I'm fine. I'll see you tomorrow."

Emma poured black coffee for herself and her bandmates. The three of them were planning to spend the day rehearsing in the shed.

"Thanks for coming to see Sid," said Anika. She yawned.

"No problem," replied Nicki. "I just wish—"

"You're knackered, Anika," said Emma, interrupting. "You look terrible."

"I wish there was something I could do to help," said Nicki.

"Unless you've got enough cash to retain a decent attorney, there's nothing you can do," said Emma. Anika gave her an admonishing glance and Emma caught herself. "Um, it was good of you to visit Sid."

Was that an apology? wondered Nicki.

She noticed a slogan on Anika's coffee mug. "None for the Road," she read aloud.

"Got it from the bar where we have most of our gigs," said Anika. "I used to work the night shift there, slinging beer."

"They start handing out coffee when they figure everyone's had enough," Dawn explained.

Anika frowned. "I hated that job. Now, I'd give anything to have it back."

Emma said nothing but had been staring at Nicki for an uncomfortably long time.

Anika noticed and broke in. "How about some caffeine, Yin? After that workout, you need it." She shook her head. "You should see her," she told her friends. "I just caught the tail end of it, but she tells me it's a daily regime. Two hours of torture every morning."

Nicki went to the refrigerator. "No thanks, I'll just have some milk."

"All out," said Emma. "Till I get paid. Two of my students owe me a fistful of dot and dash."

"Dot and dash?" asked Nicki. *Okay,* she thought, *that's cockney rhyming slang for...* "Cash?"

"I teach guitar for a living," said Emma. "If you can call it that."

"I hope the check I gave you is enough to cover my room and board. If not, I can—"

"It's enough," said Emma. She looked away.

Nicki found a carton of orange juice, poured the dregs into a glass, then shoved a piece of bread into the toaster. She turned to the drummer.

"Dawn, you said you're from Kenya, but you have a British accent."

"I was born there, but my parents moved to England when I was very young. I grew up in the East End near these two clowns." She laughed. "You hang around them long enough, you'll start speakin' with a cockney twang yourself."

Nicki smiled. "The East End, eh? Apparently Todd Bead hangs out at the meth clinic there," she said. "Do you know where it is? I want to give him his phone."

"Who cares if he ever gets it back? That guy is trouble— look what he's done to Sid," said Anika.

"The clinic's not far from my flat," said Dawn. "There's a tunnel on Belden where it crosses Merklen Street."

Emma interjected. "Listen, you should just steer clear of

Belden Street, okay? You clean-cut wholesome types wouldn't be welcome there." She sneered at Nicki.

And I thought she was finally warming up to me. Nicki picked up her toast and sat down at the table.

Dawn made an attempt to drill a hole in the wall of ice Emma had put up between herself and her new boarder. "So, how old are you, Yin?" she asked.

"Sixteen."

Emma abruptly set down her coffee and stood up. "What do you care how old she is?" She pushed her chair in to the table. "Time to start practicing." She dashed out the kitchen door and slammed it shut.

Anika ran after her.

Nicki stared at her toast. "Did I say something wrong?"

"Look, Yin," said Dawn, "since you're going to be living here a while, I might as well give it to you straight up." She reached for the coffee pot and filled her mug. "Emma's daughter, Patti, died last year. So, well, she lashes out from time to time."

"Oh, I'm sorry," said Nicki. "I didn't even know she had a daughter."

"Tuberculosis, it was." Dawn bit her lip.

"TB?" said Nicki. "I thought that was—"

"A thing of the past? Not in the UK," responded the drummer. "Certainly not in the East End. And it's getting worse."

No wonder Anika is so worried about Sid's cough.

"Couldn't anyone help her?" wondered Nicki.

"Emma's brother bought this place to get Patti out of the

42

city. Everyone kept saying that all she needed was fresh air," said Dawn, her eyes soft and sad. "She developed some kind of drug resistance. There wasn't a single antibiotic that worked."

The two of them were silent for a minute, then Dawn continued.

"Anyway," she said, "that's why we changed our mandate." She stuck a spoon into the sugar bowl and scraped what little was left into her mug. "I don't know how the heck we're going to do it, but somehow we're going to make sure that no other kid has to go through what Patti did. We're trying to get together enough money for a drop-in clinic. A place where people can go for help. A place where they won't feel like creeps if their tests turn up positive."

"I hope you can do it," said Nicki.

"There's such a stigma attached to TB. It's easier to hope the cough will just go away." Dawn looked at Nicki. "I don't blame Emma, but she certainly blames herself. She shouldn't, though. Other than some weight loss and a cough, Patti didn't have any warning signs."

"Which is why a drop-in center would be good," said Nicki, thinking of Sid. "How much have you raised?" she asked.

Dawn frowned and shook her head. "The kind of dives we get for our gigs—well, nobody's got any spare change after they've paid for their beer. And anything we get up front goes for equipment rental." She threw back her head and sighed. "I wish we had decent amps of our own. If we only had good amps…" She turned to Nicki. "I even have to rent my drums."

"I guess they'd be expensive to buy."

"Oh, yeah," said Dawn. "I only make enough for food and rent at my day job."

"Where's that?" asked Nicki.

"I'm a seamstress," Dawn replied. "I do the alterations at Fandango. It's a rich lady's store downtown—you know, for the plastic surgery set."

Like my mother. She shops there whenever she's in London.

"It makes Harrods look like the bargain basement," added the drummer, tipping up her mug to get the last drop. "Okay, they're waiting for me out there," she said, turning to go. "I'll be glad when Sid gets out. Without our sound man, nothing comes out right," she said.

Nicki followed the drummer out the door.

"Dawn?"

"Yeah?"

"They sell designer shoes at Fandango, right?"

"They do," answered the drummer, "but you'd never be able to afford them."

Actually, I would, but a flower seller wouldn't, thought Nicki. She pulled out her phone and brought up the photo of the redheaded vendor. *I wish I'd taken a better shot.*

"Dawn," she said, "you don't by any chance recognize this woman, do you? It's pretty blurry, but…"

The drummer glanced at the photo. "Sorry," she said, shaking her head. "Why do you ask?"

"She was acting strange—at the airport," Nicki said. "She looked kind of down on her luck, but I noticed she was wearing

Gucci shoes, so I thought, maybe…. Oh well, thanks anyway." She went back inside.

Right after the band started to play, Fenwick appeared at the door. "I wish my sister would look after those weeds," he declared. "The larkspur needs sunshine if it's ever going to bloom."

"Just the person I was hoping to see," said Nicki. She showed Fenwick the photo of the flower seller. "Do you know this woman?"

"I remember seeing her at the airport, but that's all," he said. "Why, Miss Nicki?"

"She's obviously the one who had Bead follow me." She raised an eyebrow. "And she's no flower seller, I can tell you that."

"Send a copy of that photo to my phone, will you? Something might turn up," he said. "And send me that photo of Warren as well, from Todd Bead's phone."

Nicki did as he asked, then went to put on a fresh pot of coffee for her guest.

The butler jumped up. "Allow me, please, Miss."

"No way," was her reply. "I let you get away with it in Toronto, but…"

"Thank you," said Fenwick, sitting back down. "My feet are killing me. Serving the royal family can be quite harrowing, to be sure. The palace is huge. By the end of the day I must have walked ten miles."

"I'd make you something to eat," said Nicki, "but we haven't much in the cupboards. Not until Emma gets paid."

"I'll see to it that some groceries are sent over. I can't have you—"

"Don't worry about it, Fenwick." She sat down next to the butler. "But I wish you had told me about Emma's daughter. Helps explain why she doesn't like me very much."

"Doesn't like you? Oh, you must be mistaken," he protested.

Nicki shrugged, and he tried to explain. "She's in pain. That's what it is."

He stared at the ground. "Patti was a sweet girl. Full of life," he said. "Your age exactly, Miss Nicki. You would have liked her."

"I'm sure I would have," she said. "Was Patti your mother's name?"

"Oh no, Miss," replied the butler. "Emma named her after Patti Smith. My sister tells me she's the godmother of punk rock."

"Oh," said Nicki, nodding.

"Music is my sister's life. It's all she has left," he explained. "At the end of every performance, the three of them sing a song that Emma wrote after Patti died. It's called 'Tuesday at Four.'" He sighed. "It breaks my heart to hear her sing it."

Nicki didn't have to ask what the title meant. She knew that must have been when Patti died.

"I'm sorry, Fenwick. For you and for your sister."

Neither of them said a word for a minute or two, then Nicki broke the silence. "Here's Bead's cell phone." She slid it across the table.

"I'll take this to a good friend at Q branch right away."

"You mean, there really is a Q?" asked Nicki. She felt a little thrill every time she was reminded of how her world now resembled that of James Bond.

"Yes, there really is a Q branch," replied the butler. "And the people involved with it are excellent eavesdroppers."

They were so engrossed in the matter of Bead's phone, neither Nicki nor the butler realized that Emma was standing right outside the screen door.

"Eavesdroppers? Eavesdropping on who?"

Chapter Six

"Emma, dear," said Fenwick, getting out of his chair to greet his sister. "How are you? You look terrific, by the way. Terrific."

"Cut the crap, Willie." She took a good look at him. "What are you up to?"

"Up to? I drove out here to see my baby sister, that's all. Now what's wrong with that?"

"Nothing, I guess. I haven't seen you in six months and you pick a day when I've got the band together to rehearse." She threw up her hands. "And we've got a gig tonight!"

Nicki poured Fenwick's coffee and offered one to Emma, but she had only come back inside to find a special guitar pick. She started searching through drawers.

"Here it is," she said. "Willie, can you stick around a while? We'll be taking a break shortly, and I—"

"Sorry, Emma," replied Fenwick. "I can't stay. But I will see you soon, I promise."

"Yeah, sure. Promises, promises." She scowled. "You hate our music."

"I do not," protested the butler.

"Yes, you do."

"Well," he said, "I must admit, I am more of a Beethoven kind of chap, but—"

"Will you come and see us play tonight?" Emma pleaded.

"You're not still at that horrible pub with the bowls of stale peanuts. What's it called?" he asked, looking into the empty sugar bowl. He sighed and shoved it back into the middle of the table.

"The Coronation House. It's not all that bad," said Emma. "They do serve dinner there." Then she changed her mind. "Okay, it is that bad. But we're going to get a better place one day. Somebody's going to hear how good we are."

"I hope you're right," said Fenwick. He turned to Nicki. "They're raising money for a drop-in center. They're doing it for—" Fenwick stopped and looked at his sister.

She said nothing, just checked to be sure she had the right pick, then headed out the door.

"Maybe it was a bad idea having you stay here," said the butler. "I guess I was hoping that—"

"That she might make me forget Patti?" Emma stormed back into the kitchen. "Not going to happen."

"Of course not," said Fenwick. "I just thought that—"

"Stop thinking," Emma snarled.

"Emma," said Nicki, "I really don't—"

"Yin," Fenwick interrupted. "Can I tell my sister about what happened to you in China?"

"Of course," said Nicki, but Emma was on her way out the door, pointedly ignoring them.

"I'm sorry about my sister's behavior," said the butler once he heard the door to the shed bang shut. "It's been so difficult…"

"I understand," said Nicki.

"Thank you," he said.

He sipped his coffee, and Nicki took note of his right hand. She had wanted to ask him how he'd lost part of his first finger, but the time never seemed right. *Did someone torture him for information?*

She was about to ask, when Fenwick began to give her instructions for finding his friend at SIS headquarters. "Bobby—our Q—will be expecting you," he said. "I wish I could drive you there myself, but as you know—"

"That's okay, Fenwick. How much time will they need to bug Bead's cell?"

"Not long. The phone will be ready for you"—he looked at his watch—"by the lunch hour, I should think."

"Good, that will give me time to get it to Bead and still make it to Mr. Letch's lecture this afternoon." She smiled. "It's pretty cool to see how closely you guys are able to keep tabs on criminals. One surveillance camera even zoomed in on a ticket that Xavier Zidane had in his hand. Oddly enough, it was for a lecture at the Natural History Museum."

"Yes, we were expecting to see him the following week, at the next lecture, but he disappeared. Vanished into thin air."

"Vanished?"

"At the House of Wax," replied the butler.

"Madame Tussaud's?" asked Nicki.

"Yes, that's right. Did you know one of the owners is a plastic surgeon?" Fenwick chuckled. "He probably tries out his surgical techniques on the wax figures first."

"Actually," said Nicki, "I remember reading that it was a physician who started Madame Tussaud's, doing the sculptures in the first place. Back in the 1700s."

"Makes sense," said the butler. "At any rate, a surveillance camera caught Zidane going in, but he avoided detection on the way out. We believe that he had his face altered." Fenwick drank the last of his coffee.

"Where is he now?" Nicki asked.

"We think he's in France, based on information from his cell phone provider, but we haven't had a positive sighting. He's on a watch list at both Heathrow and Calais, but he slipped by and we've lost track of him." The butler carried his mug to the sink. "It would be easy enough for him to get a phony passport made, but he never would have made it past the facial recognition software unless he'd had plastic surgery."

"Don't you think it's odd that he was at the Natural History Museum?" Nicki asked.

"No, that's not odd," said Fenwick.

"It isn't?"

"The lecture series is on the history and cultivation of opium poppies."

★　★　★

The entrance to the Vauxhall Bridge headquarters of the Secret Intelligence Service, an area of high potential threat for terrorism, was situated on the opposite side of the Thames, where the government buildings are located. The access to Q branch began at an otherwise normal-looking bus station—normal except that it housed a doorway behind mirrored glass. Once her iris was scanned and her card swiped, Nicki followed a narrow tunnel underneath the river and wound up in the basement of the SIS building, where inch-thick lead walls formed a fortress around the mainframe computers.

An older woman, with gray hair and a cane, greeted Nicki once she'd made it into the high security area.

"Fu Yin?" she asked.

"Yes, are you special agent Q?"

"Call me Bobby." She smiled. "At least when the boss isn't around." She entered a code onto a numeric pad to unlock the door to a filing cabinet and pulled out Bead's phone. She handed it to Nicki and explained how everything was going to work.

"We will know every move Mr. Bead makes. And not only will we have access to his calls and texts, the microphone will let us eavesdrop on his conversations, even when the phone is not in use."

"What if he turns it off?"

"This technique utilizes what we call a roving bug. It functions whether the phone is powered on or off. As long as he doesn't remove the battery, we can listen in on his nearby conversations."

"Let's hope this can lead us to Xavier Zidane."

"Indeed. We're grateful you brought us the phone, Yin. I understand that Sid Jabbar hasn't told you anything about his own connection to Zidane. Is that right?"

"I doubt he has any connection at all. He was only assisting his friend Bead—an addict he's trying to help get clean," Nicki explained. "What I don't understand is why Scotland Yard would arrest Sid and not Todd Bead with him."

"Could be they haven't enough evidence," said Bobby. "After all, they do have a shot of Sid Jabbar taking dirty money out of an automated teller. On the other hand, perhaps they want to watch Bead. Follow him to the bigger fish."

"Doesn't Scotland Yard let you in on what they're doing?"

"We share information when it becomes necessary, but until it's time for an arrest, the two agencies work alone. It's safer that way."

"If we can find Xavier Zidane and prove that he's been paying young men from the East End to commit crimes, will Sid be released from prison?" asked Nicki. "Or at least be offered some kind of leniency?"

"Well, it's not up to the secret service to determine his punishment. But if we can find Zidane, it would make a big difference, that's for sure. Zidane is the one we want. He supplies the market with more illicit drugs than anyone. He's got to be stopped."

"What do we need to prove he's guilty?" asked Nicki.

"We know he's got drugs stashed somewhere in the UK," replied Bobby. "All we have to do is find them."

★ ★ ★

"I figured you'd have handed it over to the cops by now," said Bead, turning the phone on to be sure it was his. He checked the photos, and other than Nicki's, they were all there.

"Why would I do that?" said Nicki. "Especially with the way they've been treating Sid."

"Are you his girlfriend now?"

Nicki didn't answer the question—she posed one instead.

"Was Patti his girlfriend?"

"No!" His expression changed and he looked at the ground. "They were like brother and sister." He plunked himself down on a bench in front of the meth clinic.

Nicki sat next to him. "And you—you're supposed to be Sid's best friend," she said. "But look how you've treated him. You should be ashamed of yourself."

"It's not my fault!" he said.

"You must have known they'd check the security camera and match it to the withdrawal." She paused. "In fact, it kinda seems like you set him up to take the rap for you."

"I didn't! Sid's my friend. You—who do you think you are?" His face turned bright red and sweaty. "They told me the card couldn't be traced!"

"*Who* told you?"

He said nothing.

"If that's true, then why didn't *you* make the withdrawal?" demanded Nicki.

"Because someone could have been watching. They weren't looking for Sid; it's me they want."

"Who wants you?" asked Nicki.

"Look, I don't know what your game is, but leave me alone, okay?"

Nicki saw that his hands were trembling—twitching, even.

"How's your treatment going?" she asked.

"What do you care?"

"I don't like to see anyone suffer a drug addiction. Besides, it only serves to make drug lords and mob leaders very rich."

"That your lecture for today?"

"Who is that woman at the airport, Todd? Come on, I gave you a break the other night. I didn't call the cops, and I could have, you know."

Bead offered no reply.

"This woman—she pays you to follow people?"

"I've got nothing to say." Bead got up, took another look at his phone, then headed into the clinic. He quickly changed his mind, though, and bolted back out the door and down the street.

Poor Todd, thought Nicki. *He's a mess.* She looked through the dirty plate glass window at the lineups of men and women, waiting to swallow a glass of orange juice and methadone. There were teenagers, younger than herself, people in their twenties and thirties, and a few much older than that. Their faces exhibited pain, fear, shame.

She took a shortcut to the former sugar factory, past some of the worst looking, most crowded homes she'd ever seen. The roofs were in such bad shape that some of the beams were exposed, and many had been patched with cardboard and plastic. Kids in various stages of undress played with whatever they could find in the alley. A middle-aged man, sitting on a crate near a crosswalk, held out a sign that read "Unemployed. Three Children. Will work for food." Nicki gave him everything she had in her wallet.

Pulling open the black fire escape doors, she thought for a minute about her parents in China.

They must have been destitute themselves, or they wouldn't have left me on the road.

The door closed behind her, and as she made her way to the classroom, she promised herself that one day—somehow—she would provide for them.

Chapter Seven

Warren Letch let out a big laugh when Nicki mentioned CSIS, the Canadian Security Intelligence Service. She was among the group of students who had joined him for coffee in the vending machine area once classes had ended for the day. Nicki thought she would take the opportunity to get to know her teacher better; now she wished she hadn't bothered.

"I'm sorry," he said, in a tone that meant *I'm not really, but I'll say it anyway*, "it's just that CSIS is somewhat of a joke around here."

Two of her fellow students, both men in their early thirties, snickered to themselves. Nicki became defensive.

"We have a good system in Canada, and the RCMP—"

"When it comes to Canada, your intelligence agency operates in a purely defensive mode, for heaven's sake. In today's world, every country needs a foreign intelligence service, one that aggressively seeks out information. We've been telling the Canadian government that for years. And when they finally agree that they need some assertive intelligence gathering, CSIS picks a girl, a sixteen-year-old girl to be their first foreign operative?" He laughed out loud again. "Oh, please."

Nicki was used to being underestimated. It often gave her an advantage over opponents. *Just you wait and see*, she thought.

"Look," said Letch, "I have nothing against you personally, okay?" He looked at the clock on the wall, then took a bottle of prescription medication from his briefcase, carefully shook out one of the tiny pills, and popped it into his mouth. Nicki read the side of the container: Lanoxin .125 mg. He followed her gaze, then mumbled something about a heart condition.

"Mr. Letch," said Nicki, trying to put his unkind remarks behind her, "you showed us a picture of Xavier Zidane, and among his contacts was a young man named Sid Jabbar. How exactly are they connected?"

Letch stood up and his eyes flashed.

"Zidane is way out of your league, believe me. Our best assets can't get a line on him. You're still a student. Remember that."

"What about 'follow the money,'" asked a young man. "Didn't you say that was the way to track down members of a syndicate?"

"Yes. In this case, we don't know yet how he's laundering such large amounts of cash. But we'll find out." He crushed his coffee cup in his hand, then turned to Nicki. "Leave Zidane to me."

Nicki made her way to the Whitechapel area of East London and found the Coronation House at the corner of two narrow streets. Above the bar were several floors of rooms for rent; the dingy curtains that hung in the windows swayed back and forth in the struggling evening breeze. Two women stood at the entrance to the bar, arguing about a guy. They were so busy hollering at each other, they failed to see that Nicki was trying to get past. When one of them finally noticed her, she stopped on the spot.

"What's your problem?" she snapped, almost losing her gum in the process.

Nicki ignored her and pushed by. She strode into the bar and chose a spot close to where the band was setting up. With Sid in jail, the women were scrambling to assemble their equipment against the back wall of the pub.

"Where does this thing go?" hollered Emma, dragging a ten-foot extension cord behind her. "It must go here," she said, plugging it into a large amp. Several sparks flew out and the cord started to smoke. She yanked it out. "Dawn, where the—where does this thing go?"

"Let me help," said Nicki. She lifted up what looked like a breaker panel of some sort.

"Sit down," barked Emma. "I don't know how we're going

to get this junk set up in time without Sid here, but you're no help at all." She headed to the hall to carry in more gear.

Dawn, obviously used to running interference for Emma's moods, came over to talk to Nicki. "We've been relying heavily on Sid to handle the rental equipment. We're lost without him," she said.

"Any news about him? Is his cough getting any better?" Nicki asked. She glanced over at Anika, who was plugging in her guitar.

"Don't know," Dawn replied in a whisper. "Frankly, I'm afraid to ask."

Nicki nodded. "Do you always play on Thursday nights?" she asked.

"We play whenever they'll let us," replied Dawn. "They usually reserve Fridays and Saturdays for bigger name bands."

"I think your band is great. Who are these other bands?"

"They're no better than us, really," she said. "Some of them aren't as good. But it's not *what* you know it's *who* you know, right?"

Nicki nodded again as a waitress swiped a grimy rag across the table in front of her, threw down a glass of warm tap water and a menu, and said, "Nothing to drink but water or soda for you."

The laminated menu featured deep-fried cheese balls, sausage-wrapped Scotch eggs, and something called bangers and mash—little for a health-conscious vegetarian like Nicki. When she ordered a salad, the waitress looked at her as if she'd asked for rat-on-a-stick, and when Nicki asked if they had dill pickles—she loved pickles—the woman simply stared.

The salad, when it arrived, was nothing more than a few wilted leaves of last week's lettuce, smothered in dressing, and tasted like someone had taken grass and covered it in machine oil. And Nicki had to use a spoon and knife to eat it; the fork she'd been given had something stuck on it.

The music more than made up for the food. The Leather Daisies were very talented musicians, and Nicki enjoyed listening to punk rock live and from only a few feet away. It was loud and more confrontational than anything she'd ever heard before, but it offered an authentic taste of a London she'd never experienced.

The band's outfits were wild—thick red and blue stripes on a white background—and when they stood side by side, the lines formed the Union Jack. Nicki figured Dawn must have designed them.

Nicki applauded enthusiastically after each number, but no one else in the bar joined her. They stayed glued to their conversations, drank their beer, and acted as if they hadn't heard a thing.

What a total waste of talent, thought Nicki. *These people should be on their feet cheering.*

"Thank you," said Emma into the microphone, then she introduced her band members. Apparently undaunted by the complete lack of attention they'd received from the audience, she announced their next song—an original tune, written by Emma herself, about the grim realities of growing up in the East End.

Wow, she's got great stage presence, and she's a good songwriter, too, Nicki thought. She was lost in the song when she felt a hand touch her back. She started and turned to see a man in a black jacket, black trousers and a hat pulled down over his forehead.

"What is it?" she demanded. "What do you—Fenwick!"

He turned without speaking, indicating she should follow. He led her to an empty corner of the pub where they could talk without being overheard.

"Emma will be glad you came," said Nicki. "Her band is really good. It's a shame the audience—"

"Yes, Miss Nicki, you're quite right. Sorry to interrupt, but I have only a few minutes," he said. "I'm on my way to Windsor Castle."

"Windsor Castle?"

"That's what I came to tell you. I haven't got long, so you must listen carefully."

A waiter tried to squeeze between them to get a carton of potato chips. Nicki moved aside to let him by. Once he'd left, the two of them resumed their conversation.

"No one can hear us over the music," Nicki said, looking around to be sure they were alone. "What is it, Fenwick?"

"Bobby and her team have picked up some activity from Mr. Bead's cell phone. They've been listening to his conversations with fellow gang members."

"What did they learn?"

"Unfortunately, this group of young—well, I want to say thugs, but that's too weak a word. Anyway, this Belden Street Gang spends a lot of time in the Merklen tunnel, so it's difficult to hear them over the background traffic noise. The conversations indicate that they are working for the syndicate, that's for certain. The mob has provided them with damaging information about many of our agents."

"Bead had you pegged as a cop," said Nicki. "Maybe that flower seller recognized you from somewhere, Fenwick. Maybe she thinks you're with Scotland Yard." The waiter reappeared and she moved aside so he could reach a box of serviettes. "Are you sure you don't know who she is?"

"I've looked at the photo you sent many times, Miss Nicki, but I'm certain I've never seen the woman before the airport."

Nicki sighed. "So where does Windsor Castle fit into all of this?"

"Todd Bead received an encrypted text message, and the sender identified himself as XZZ. That message came from a server in France, Miss Nicki," said Fenwick.

"Xavier Zidane."

"Most likely."

"What's the extra Z for?" wondered Nicki.

"We don't know."

"Were the code breakers able to decipher the message?" she asked.

"The text instructed these young men to tour Windsor Castle on Saturday." He shook his head in disbelief. "As for what they're planning to do there, we don't have a clue. Perhaps another message will follow."

"Isn't Windsor Castle a private home for the royal family?" asked Nicki.

"Of sorts. They use it for entertaining politicians and public figures."

"Could that be it? Are they going to kidnap someone?"

"No. There is nothing scheduled for Saturday other than a tour of the library and archives." He shrugged again. "There are some coins and medals dating from the time of Queen Victoria, but again, hardly the kind of thing a man like Xavier Zidane would be after."

"Not worth his time," added Nicki. "But then I can't imagine him sitting through a lecture at the Natural History Museum either—even if it is about poppies."

The butler nodded.

"When is the next lecture in that series?" Nicki asked.

"Tomorrow night. But he won't be there, Nicki. He's long gone."

Nicki folded her arms across her chest. "I'm going anyway."

"To the lecture?"

"Yes."

"Miss Nicki, if anyone from the syndicate spots you at the lecture, Bead will no doubt be notified. If you lose your cover, we'll lose our access to the Belden Street Gang."

"I want to see what these lectures are about," said Nicki. "There must be something there that Zidane wants. I mean, you can find out everything there is to know about poppy plants and opium on the Internet, right?"

The butler nodded, then checked his watch.

"I've got to be at Windsor Castle in half an hour," he said. "I'll be in touch."

Nicki stuck her hand in a bowl of peanuts on a nearby table.

"Oh, and Miss Nicki?" added Fenwick. "A word of advice—"

"What's that?"

"Don't eat those peanuts," he said.

Chapter Eight

A fog had descended upon Milchester the next day, so thick that when Nicki took her morning run through the streets of the town, it was as if the day had never dawned. She saw a light burning in the kitchen of an early riser, watching out the window as she strode past.

Her mind was usually clear at that time of the morning, but when she thought about Xavier Zidane and his appearance at the lecture, nothing made sense.

What was he doing at those lectures? And what is it that he expects the gang members to find tomorrow at Windsor Castle?

Trying to shake these questions out of her mind was like trying to swim at the edge of a whirlpool, and even the bus trip into the city was spent mulling over the events of the previous three days.

Mr. Letch had taken the day to work on a current investigation, so guest speakers took over the classes. They taught everything from traditional methods of espionage to the difference between confidential, secret, and top secret information.

One speaker mentioned Canada and how Canadian technology, especially its nuclear technology, is vital around the world and why it is important for the research from Canadian universities and corporations to be protected. She couldn't help feeling proud that the Canadian government believed she could be of service to the nation. She was more determined than ever to show Letch that CSIS had chosen wisely.

The last class of the day was on money laundering and the techniques that criminals use—commingling, layering, and structuring.

"In the case of commingling, a cash-intensive business is used to blend the proceeds of illicit drug sales with those of the legitimate business," said the instructor. "Layering involves international wire transfers being used to buy cashier's checks, which are then deposited in someone else's name. While large transfers of ten thousand dollars or more are spotted by SIS computers," she explained, "members of organized crime find ways to send numerous wire transfers abroad that remain under the reporting threshold."

Nicki raised her hand. "So if Xavier Zidane uses these techniques to launder the proceeds of his drug money, how can we ever hope to arrest him?" she asked, and everyone in the room laughed.

Why are they laughing at me? she wondered.

The instructor quickly gave her the answer.

"I realize you're a rookie, 7347, but the secret service has no powers of arrest. Only Scotland Yard can *arrest* someone."

Oh yeah. I knew that, thought Nicki. She looked sheepishly at the guy beside her and he grinned.

Lesson learned. Think before you speak.

★　★　★

It was late in the afternoon when she left the school and took the tube to South Kensington. Rather than head directly to the Natural History Museum, she decided to go first to the White Tiger Martial Arts Academy to find a sparring partner. Grand Master Kahana had recommended it for practice while she was in London. It wasn't far from the museum and would give her a chance to work off some of the embarrassment she carried with her out of the classroom.

She looked down at her shorts. *I'd rather wear my cotton uniform. I've got one in our penthouse at Haddon Gardens. No one will spot me if I slip in and out.*

As she made her way to the hotel, she passed by Fandango and gazed through the glass. Women strolled in and out wearing Versace and Chanel and self-satisfied smiles. Nicki looked around for Dawn but didn't see her.

One of the sales clerks gave her a dirty look through the window. Although her parents could easily buy her every single item in the shop, Nicki just smiled and went on her way. She turned down the next side street and took the staff entrance into the hotel. She hopped onto a service elevator and rode thirty floors into the air. She moved quickly from the elevator door to the penthouse. Just as she entered the code that would unlock the door, a voice rang out behind her.

"Nicki! Is that you?"

It was her father. He gave her a big hug.

"Dad! I thought you were in Paris."

"I was, but they needed me here to sign some papers. I'll be around until tomorrow, and then I'm meeting your mother back in Toronto. I tried to reach you twice today, but your phone was turned off. I guess you were—"

"Working out," Nicki said quickly.

He swung open the door, and Nicki threw her duffel bag down onto the white broadloom.

"Gosh, it's good to see you," said her father. "I haven't had a chance to chat with you in ages." He took off his jacket and hung it in the closet. "Let's have supper together tonight in the Starlight Room."

The Starlight Room, located in a domed atrium on the roof of Haddon Gardens—complete with blossoming orange trees and a patio with potted palms—had the best food in the city, not to mention a magnificent view. Although the meals were wonderful, Nicki usually preferred the club downstairs called The Zone. Just as upscale as the Starlight Room but geared to a younger crowd, The Zone was a trendy place where popular bands played every night of the week.

But Nicki didn't want to go there. Not now.

"Uh, Dad," said Nicki. "I was just going to have a quick

workout at the White Tiger Academy. I haven't had much time for my—"

"I thought you were working out every day at the special school for elite athletes."

Oh! Right! Of course! Where's my head today?

"Yes, Dad. That's true," said Nicki, fumbling through her duffel bag. "But there is an expert in swords at this place, and I thought I'd take the opportunity to spar with him."

I hate lying to my father. Hate it.

"But Nicki," said Mr. Haddon, "I have to leave tomorrow. I might not see you for another month or more. Please have supper with your old dad, won't you?"

Nicki couldn't get out of it. On the one hand, she was happy to see her father, but on the other, she knew that the lecture at the museum was in just an hour and a half.

"I'll tell you what," said Nicki, opening up the doors to the terrace. "The view from here is every bit as nice as the one from the restaurant, but we can be quiet and away from the crowds." She smiled at her father.

"But it's about to rain, Nicki," argued Mr. Haddon. He joined her outside. "In fact, it is raining!" He held up his hand to catch the drops.

"Well, we can order room service and eat here in the dining room." She ushered him back inside and pulled the doors closed.

"Fine," said Mr. Haddon, "as long as I get to spend some time with my daughter, I really don't care where we eat." He picked up the phone. "What would you like, Nicki?"

"A salad! Please! Anything with fresh vegetables and nuts and fruit and maybe—"

"A Waldorf salad, please," said her father into the phone. "Make that two, and how about some stuffed avocados and rosemary bread. For dessert—"

Nicki shook her head.

"Send up a chocolate truffle mousse, will you? And two spoons."

Nicki smiled. "Dad, I don't want dessert."

"You're too thin, Nicki. You need to put on some weight."

Nicki jumped out of the chair and showed him how many one-handed push-ups she could do without even breaking a sweat.

"All right, all right," laughed Mr. Haddon. "You're fit, I get it. I won't make you eat the mousse."

Nicki sat down next to her dad. "Well, maybe I'll have a little bit."

"Good," he said. "I'm glad you're here, Nicki." He thought for a minute. "I guess you would have preferred to have dinner at The Zone," he said. "It's too loud for me, but—"

"I'm happy here."

"Excellent. You know, speaking of The Zone, there's a new manager at the club. She's got some good ideas for the place."

"It's doing well, isn't it?"

"Oh, yes. Very popular place. But fresh ideas can never hurt, right?"

Absolutely, thought Nicki. *The Zone could use some new energy.*

They settled into a comfortable conversation and before long, a waiter knocked on the door and pushed in a cart, over which was draped an Irish linen tablecloth. A white rose in a slim crystal vase graced the middle, and highly polished silverware surrounded the Royal Doulton chinaware.

When her father went into the hallway to talk to the waiter, Nicki slipped into the master bedroom. Mrs. Haddon had many wigs in her collection; Nicki chose a short red one and stuffed it into her duffle bag. *She doesn't like this one anyway*, she reasoned. She was back at the table before her dad even noticed she'd left.

Nicki dove into her salad.

"Haven't they been feeding you at the martial arts academy?" asked her father. "David Kahana assured us that—"

"Oh sure, Dad. Everything's great. But let's face it, it's not every day I can have a cordon bleu chef making my meals."

Mr. Haddon laughed. "I guess that's true. Anytime you want something decent, have Fenwick bring you over." He smiled. "But I guess you like to eat with your friends."

Then his expression changed.

"Speaking of David Kahana, Nicki," he said, "I've been wanting to talk to you about something."

"Is something wrong?"

"No, nothing's wrong," he replied. "But your Grand Master called me when I was in Paris. He had a lot of questions."

"Questions?"

"About your adoption, Nicki." Mr. Haddon poured himself a cup of coffee. "I contacted your mother in Toronto and she said that you were okay with it, so I did my best to give him the answers he needed."

"I asked him to help me, Dad." Nicki felt herself tremble a bit when she spoke. She wondered how her father would feel, knowing that she wanted to find her birth parents. "You see, he's going to China, and I was hoping that he could—"

"That he could put you in touch with your real—"

"Not *real*, Dad. You are my real father. You and Mom are my real parents." She struggled to find the words to express what she felt inside. "It's just that I would like to meet the people who left me. Find out why they did it." She looked down as she fingered the charm around her neck. "Find out why they left me on the road like that."

"I'm sure they had no choice, Nicki. No choice whatsoever."

Nicki went to take another bite then set down her fork.

"I hope they're not hungry. I can't stand thinking that they're hungry."

Mr. Haddon also set down his fork. "David Kahana asked me very pointed questions, Nicki, about the orphanage from which we adopted you, the papers we signed, and the people we talked to during the entire process. I have a pretty good memory, but—"

"I'm sure you did your best, Dad. And I am grateful for that." She was still fingering her charm.

"I see you still have that pendant," said Mr. Haddon. He smiled. "Your mother and I have bought you emeralds and sapphires, but that inexpensive little metal charm means more to you than any of them, doesn't it?"

"It does," said Nicki.
It does.

Chapter Nine

So involved was Nicki in her conversation with her father, she completely lost track of time and was already a half hour late for the lecture before she noticed. The museum wasn't far from the hotel, so she made her way there on foot, despite the rain, making a quick stop at a nearby cafe to change clothes and pull on her wig in the restroom. When she hit the front entrance of the huge Romanesque structure, she could hardly believe her eyes.

Two emergency vehicles—a police car and an ambulance—had pulled up to the front door, and while their flashing lights beamed streams of color through the rain, emergency attendants hollered at the crowd to stay back. Nicki quickly scanned people's faces, which wasn't easy since everyone was huddled under umbrellas, but she saw no one who resembled Xavier Zidane.

The paramedics carried a man out on a stretcher. He was pale, white even, and they were pumping away at his heart. There was no sign of blood, so Nicki assumed he must have had a heart attack.

She ran around the building until she found another entrance. Once inside, she combed the corridors, searching for Zidane. She found nothing but empty halls, except for a janitor, and he didn't know anything about what had happened.

Nicki came upon a group of people standing outside an office door. The sign said "Sir Richard Spring, PhD, Superintendent, Natural History Collection." A man left the crowd and headed toward the back door, and Nicki ran behind him.

"Mr. Letch!"

He turned automatically, then quickly scanned to see if anyone had heard her. "Who are you?" he demanded.

"It's me," she whispered, turning up a corner of the wig to reveal her own dark hair.

"Good god, girl!" he hissed. If looks could kill, he'd have murdered Nicki.

"Oh," she slapped her hand on her mouth. *I can't believe I used his real name in public!*

"You've mistaken me for someone else," he said. He spun back around and continued down the hall. Nicki watched as he picked up his pace, crashed through a back door, and headed out into the parking lot.

Why is he in such a hurry? She gave herself a mental lashing for potentially blowing Letch's cover, then made her way back to the office of the superintendent and started up a conversation with an older couple.

"Do you know what happened?" she asked them. "Who is the man they carried out on a stretcher?"

"Sir Richard, our lecturer," replied the woman.

"Heart attack," said her husband. "That's what they think."

"Oh, it was horrible," said the woman. "We were enjoying some refreshments and chatting about flowers, and then he fell down. His coffee and all of his lecture notes flew right out of his hands."

"Oh dear," said Nicki. "What a shame."

"It's a good thing there was a physician on hand," said the man. "He was right there, chatting with Sir Richard when it happened."

"A physician?" Nicki asked.

"Yes," he replied. "So he knew right away that it was a heart attack."

Nicki asked the couple if they knew the doctor's name, but they didn't. "So Sir Richard collapsed *before* his lecture?" she asked.

"That's right," said the man. "A pity too, as this was the final night in his lecture series. Oh, I do hope he survives the attack."

Nicki read the back of a folder in the man's hand. "This lecture series is on the history of poppies, correct?"

"Oh, it's been so fascinating," replied the lady. "We learned about the ancient Sumerians, and did you know that archaeologists have found fossilized poppy pods in Europe that go back four thousand years?"

"Very interesting! What else did you learn?"

"The best part was about the opium wars," said the man, "and how the Chinese imperial court wanted the flower banned from their country, to stop people from becoming addicted. They even petitioned Queen Victoria to ask the British government to stop importing opium from India into China, but were ignored."

"And then, in 1880, her grandsons traveled to the Orient on the HMS *Bacchante*, and—how did that go, dear?" the woman asked her husband.

"Well, it seems that they visited some intriguing people while in China, and Sir Richard said that one old fellow—a Buddhist monk, I think he said—was so sure the imperial court was going to destroy his poppy plants, that he begged the two princes to ask their grandmother for help. I guess he figured she might be able to protect the plants somehow."

"That's right," agreed the woman. "But here's the interesting part—"

"Interesting part?" asked Nicki.

"The flowers that he grew were not ordinary," she said. "No, this monk had developed a special golden poppy. He'd spent many years of his life, working with various strains of *papaver somniferum*."

"Poppies are usually pink or red, sometimes white," interjected the man.

"But this poppy was yellow. And Sir Richard said that the potency of this plant was fifty times that of an ordinary poppy."

"Fifty times?" gasped Nicki. "Is that why the monk created it—for opium?"

"Oh, good heavens, no," said the woman. "He was only interested in the beauty of the golden flower. It holds great significance in China."

Nicki thought of the many paintings of Chinese flowers her mother had hung to remind Nicki of her heritage in a country so far away. They were simple drawings, with only a touch of color, but therein lay the perfection. She understood what the woman was saying, that the flower itself was the important thing.

"Did Sir Richard say what happened to the plants? Did the princes take them back to England?" Nicki asked.

"He was just getting to that part," said the woman. "That was to be our lecture tonight. All he told us last week was that the story involved a book."

A book! So that's why the syndicate is going to hit Windsor Castle and the royal library!

"Did he say what book?"

"No, he didn't." The woman smiled. "He said that the princes returned from China with a very special book and that it was connected to the poppy somehow."

Her husband looked up at the huge domed ceiling. "I love this place. It's old, you know. Darwin himself collected specimens that are in here. Of course, the museum is renowned for its exhibition of dinosaur skeletons, but it also has a huge seed collection and a world-famous botany department that has specimens from as far back as the voyages of Captain James Cook."

His wife broke in. "Sir Richard had been organizing the archives in the basement a few weeks back. That's how he stumbled upon a file made by a former superintendent who had met with Victoria and learned of the golden poppy. Tonight he was going to finish telling us all about it."

"And Sir Richard had copies of this file in his notes?" asked Nicki.

"I guess so." The man pointed to the people in a nearby lobby. "It's a shame he never got to complete his lecture series. This is the biggest turnout the museum has ever had."

"So these lectures were advertised?"

"Yes, there was an article in the newspaper," he replied. "Sir Richard didn't give the whole story away, but he invited the press to be here tonight to hear what he'd discovered."

Nicki's mind was abuzz. She knew the key to uncovering the smuggling ring was at hand, if only she could put the pieces together.

"Thank you both, so much. It's been a pleasure speaking with you," she said. "I hope that Sir Richard has a speedy recovery."

"So do we."

"Oh, one more thing," added Nicki. "When Sir Richard collapsed, what happened to his lecture notes?"

"Let me think," said the woman, but her husband answered for her.

"It must have been that physician. Yes, he picked up the notes after he tried to revive Sir Richard." He looked puzzled. "I don't know what he did with them after that."

Chapter Ten

Nicki spent Saturday morning sparring with other black belts at the White Tiger Martial Arts Academy. She never allowed a full week to pass without a complete workout. She could keep physically fit by running, but interaction with other martial artists was key to her kung fu practice.

Grand Master Kahana had recommended this school because it specialized in Wing Chun, which differs from other wushu techniques in that it's less stylistic, while remaining devastatingly effective as a fighting art. Nicki practiced her kicks and punches, and an instructor helped tone her pivots, which are important when one must move quickly and redirect force in opposite directions. She worked on her stance, too. Unlike other kung fu styles, the Wing Chun stance can appear to the opponent like a natural position when in fact you are ready to fight.

"Great, Yin," hollered her instructor. "Watch your center line." They continued sparring, and Nicki was grateful to have a chance to practice with a partner who worked at her level. "Thrust your knuckles forward, Yin," he said, "and that will add power to your punch."

She threw several jabs in quick succession. Known as a "straight blast," the move is used in kung fu to disorient the attacker.

"Now let's try a hammer punch," suggested the teacher, and with every successive blow, Nicki moved closer and closer, finally driving her fists forward like a hammer banging a nail.

"Excellent work, Yin."

"Thanks," she said, wiping her forehead with a towel. She bowed. "I appreciate your time today."

"Any time," he replied, bowing in return. "Come back soon and we'll work on your kicks." He smiled. "Not that they need much work. But try to keep your limbs relaxed, yet focused. You seem a bit tense."

I am tense, thought Nicki, as she headed for the change room.

It was early afternoon by that time, and since she wasn't far from the hotel, she decided she'd stop by to meet with the new manager of The Zone. First she tried calling Fenwick again—it was her third attempt—but she still couldn't get him to pick up.

The Zone was empty that time of day except for the cleaning staff and cooks getting things ready for the supper crowd. Nicki figured it would be a good time for a meeting with the manager.

"Ms. Mills?"

"Yes?" She swiveled around in her desk chair to face Nicki. "If you're looking for a job, there's a pile of application forms sitting at the end of the bar. You can fill one in and leave it with the bartender. Thanks." She looked closely at Nicki. "You're too young to serve drinks, but we are hiring busboys and girls right now, if you don't mind cleaning tables."

"Ms. Mills," replied Nicki. "I'm not here for a job. My father told me he had hired you, and I—"

The manager's face turned scarlet and she jumped out of her chair.

"I'm sorry, I thought...oh gosh, that's right. I saw your picture on his desk."

"Don't worry, honestly. But if you could give me a few minutes of your time, I'd like to talk to you about the club."

"Certainly, certainly," she said. She offered Nicki her chair, but she declined.

"What is it that you want to discuss?"

"The music."

Nicki called Fenwick again; this time she got through. She was anxious to tell him about Sir Richard, but as it turned out, he was already well aware of the events of the previous night and had some news himself about what had happened to the botanist.

"Poison?" said Nicki, whispering into her cell phone from

outside the hotel. "What kind of poison, Fenwick?"

"Heart medication of some kind. Probably digoxin. He suffered a massive coronary, and although he's expected to survive, he's in no condition to provide details to the police. Not yet, anyway."

"I spoke to some people who were there when it happened, Fenwick."

"What did you find out?"

Once Nicki had gone over everything she'd learned about the princes' trip to China, the monk, and the book, she pointed out the connection to the royal library. "That must be why Zidane is so interested in Windsor Castle," she added.

"Well, yes," said the butler, "the library houses precious manuscripts and books, to be sure. But there are thousands of them. How could a few lads possibly find one particular book during a tour?"

"Good question."

"There's something else you should know, Miss Nicki. Scotland Yard has arrested Warren Letch."

"They have? I saw him leaving the lecture last night, but—"

"They're questioning him about the poisoning of Sir Richard," declared the butler. "The crime scene investigators combed the museum lobby where refreshments were served last night before the lecture, and they found Lanoxin pills."

"Mr. Letch takes Lanoxin for his heart condition."

"It's a brand name for digoxin, Miss Nicki. They're tiny tablets, but the CSI team managed to find two of them." Fenwick took a deep breath. "From what I understand, the police received an anonymous tip, then traced the taggant back to Warren."

"Taggant?"

"Pharmaceutical companies put encoded microscopic markers in their medicines for brand protection. It's complicated, but essentially it means they can trace the pills back to a lot number."

"And the lot number matched Mr. Letch's prescription?"

"Yes, Miss Nicki."

"But why would he poison Sir Richard?" Before he had a chance to answer, she asked, "What do you think of Mr. Letch, Fenwick? Could he be working with the mob?"

"Warren is a hothead. He is the kind of agent who prefers to do things alone, without involving anyone. I guess you'd say he's arrogant. Has he any connection to organized crime? I wouldn't even hazard a guess." The butler paused. "Whenever an anonymous tip comes in, you have to wonder if someone is being framed. And those pills—"

"Too convenient, even with having to trace a taggant."

"Right," he replied. "Could be Warren was framed."

"Mr. Letch was probably there last night to see if Zidane showed up," said Nicki. "I admit, that's partly why I was there."

"You shouldn't have risked it. If someone—"

"Don't worry, Fenwick. I wore a disguise," the girl explained. Then she had a question. "Have the surveillance cameras been checked yet?"

"The Natural History Museum is a low-risk venue. At least it was until now," replied the butler. "So there are cameras at the main entrances and near some special exhibits, but that's about it. I understand that Scotland Yard has checked the tapes using facial recognition software, but nothing turned up."

"It was raining heavily, Fenwick. Everyone had umbrellas and hats. The cameras would have had a hard time capturing faces." Nicki sighed. "Too bad there wasn't a camera in the lobby where the refreshments were served. I'd have liked to get a look at the man who picked up Sir Richard's notes."

"Someone took his notes?"

"Yes," replied Nicki. "A physician."

"Interesting. We'll see if we can track him down, find out what he did with them," said Fenwick. "By the way, Miss Nicki, I am going to require the help of some undercover police officers at the castle today."

"You're not worried about involving the police?"

"I have no choice. Because the royal palace is involved, we can't take any chances. With any luck, Mr. Bead will get a text message that will help us out. If we knew the name of the book…"

"But if no message comes, the police will be ready to act if anyone tries to leave with anything," said Nicki.

"Yes, of course." A bell rang in the background, calling the butler away. "I must go, Miss Nicki. You can't be seen here at Windsor Castle. I'm serious, Miss. Stay away. We don't want Bead and his friends connecting you with our investigation. Why don't you relax at Emma's for the afternoon?"

"Relax? No, Fenwick. I have some important work to do today."

"What's that?"

"I'm heading back to Adder Street, to the school."

"There are no classes today, Miss Nicki."

"I know. I have something else in mind."

Chapter Eleven

Nicki wasn't sure if the door was programmed to remain closed on weekends, but luckily her swipe card and the iris scanner allowed her entry.

The school appeared to be vacant. The sound of her feet treading down the sealed hallway and the thick doors slamming behind her seemed so much louder than they did during the week. She gazed in through the wired glass to where the technicians receive their training, but no one was there. No one was in the lunch area either. Yet she heard voices.

Probably security guards.

She traced the voices to a room several doors down from where she stood. The door was closed, but she could tell by the tone of their conversation that they were agents working on a case. In the adjacent room, a security guard was reading a magazine; the surveillance cameras were behind his back.

Good, thought Nicki. *Maybe he didn't see me come in. If he did, I can say I left my phone here yesterday in my desk.*

Warren Letch's office was directly next to her classroom. She tried the door. It was locked. Nicki had brought a pin with her in case she had to pick the lock, but it didn't work.

They teach foreign politics and standard operating procedures and codes of behavior for every embassy and consulate on the planet. Why couldn't they also teach us something really useful, like how to pick a lock?

She'd heard somewhere that using oil helps, so she went into the washroom next to Letch's office and squirted some soap onto a piece of paper towel.

That didn't work either.

Then she had a thought. Going back into the washroom, she looked up at the ceiling and spotted a vent for the heating system. She figured it was just big enough for her to squeeze through and into the heat ducts that ran across the building. Being small in stature had its advantages.

She needed something to stand on—the toilets weren't in the right location. She went into the classroom and found a chair. It creaked a bit when she started to push it, and for a minute she thought she heard someone coming. No one did, so she picked up the chair and carried it into the washroom. The low ceiling meant Nicki could just reach the vent when she stood on tiptoe on the chair. Luckily, the vent was not screwed in; it was easily pushed out of place.

Nicki pulled herself up and peered inside the duct. She saw some light filtering in a little farther down, toward Letch's office. Gripping the ceiling on either side of the hole where the vent had been, Nicki pulled herself up and into the shaft. It was a tight fit, but she was able to shimmy along the duct. Other than dust and fibers that made her choke, the process went smoothly.

She removed the vent that she judged to be over Letch's office, then lowered herself and dropped down beside a large metal desk.

None of the drawers were locked, so she was able to do a full search. Top secret files were kept at Vauxhall Bridge headquarters, but since information from Sir Richard's lectures was not classified, she hoped to find it there.

Nicki waded through dozens of papers about her fellow students—information about their education, background, security checks. When she came to her own file, it contained only one photograph and a notation.

Fu Yin
Age 16 (D.O.B. unknown)
Canadian/American Citizen
Recruited by CSIS, CIA, and MI6

He must wonder why there is so little information about me, thought Nicki.

Letch also kept information about the members of organized crime. She found Zidane's file and went through it carefully. There were several surveillance photographs, including the most recent one from the House of Wax.

Letch has been after Zidane for weeks but doesn't know much about him at all. Seems he has no clue as to where he keeps the drugs.

Finally, in the bottom drawer, she located a folder marked "Natural History Museum Lectures." Letch had written down everything Sir Richard had said about the golden poppy, the fact that Queen Victoria's grandsons learned of its unique qualities while traveling in China, and the fact that the botanist was about to make a special announcement about something he had stumbled on in the museum archives.

Nicki turned page after page, hoping to find the title of the book. There were several scrawled notes about poppies in general, the history of the flower, and the opium wars, but nothing about the book.

Come on, what book?

She got to the end of the pages, and paper-clipped to the back of the file folder was a business card for an antiquarian book dealer.

Mr. H. Dwight Talon
Expert in Antique Books
Talon's Books
Corner Regent Street and Piccadilly, Second Floor

Nicki put the card into her pocket and carefully returned the file. She had just turned on Letch's computer, when she heard two people talking outside the door.

She froze. *They don't know I'm in here*, she reasoned.

She continued tapping away softly at the keyboard, then the door handle started to jiggle.

"When did you get the duplicate made?" asked the first man.

Oh, no. They have a key.

Nicki had no time to turn the computer off and no time to climb back into the ceiling. She hurried into a small closet, just big enough to store a coat and not much else. She pulled the door closed behind her, and not a moment too soon.

"Anyway," said the first agent, "they'll hold Letch at least until Richard Spring is well enough to identify who spiked his coffee. By then, the Zidanes will have made the transfer to Osman."

Zidanes? thought Nicki. *There's more than one?*

"Providing we find the book before Monday night," added the second man.

Nicki couldn't make out their next words, but it was clear that one of them had noticed the computer had been left on. They batted around ideas as to why, but neither one of them suspected that someone had broken into the office. Nicki prayed that they didn't look up and see that the ceiling vent had been removed.

"Okay, so let's work fast and get out of here," one of them said.

Nicki waited while they opened and closed the drawers of the desk, muttering about the contents of various files.

"Here's the notation…," she heard one agent say, but she

couldn't make out the rest of his sentence.

"You check his computer—see if you can gain access—and I'll carry on here."

For the next twenty minutes, Nicki was unable to move an inch. She listened to the men complain that the information they needed wasn't there. At first, Nicki thought that, like her, it was the title of the book they wanted.

She was wrong. They knew the name of the book. But they didn't know where it was.

"There's nothing here to help us," said one of them, sounding frustrated. "I don't think Letch knows either. Oh, come on! Where is *The Secret of the Golden Flower*?"

The Secret of the Golden Flower! That's the title!

Nicki heard a drawer slam shut. Then the rustling of papers.

"Here we go," said the first man.

"What have you got?"

The two of them were quiet for several minutes, as they paged through a file.

"...a map of the south coast and the English Channel," one of them mumbled.

The English Channel?

"Yeah, Penzance," said the other, but Nicki couldn't make out the rest of his sentence.

What about Penzance?

"Let's hope...at Windsor Castle today...." Nicki desperately tried to hear every word, but they had moved into the hall and closed the door behind them.

She crept out of the closet and over to the door, putting her ear to the crack to see if she could hear anything more.

Their words drifted off as they made their way down the hall. Nicki opened the door a tiny bit, hoping to catch a glimpse of the two men, but they had already turned the corner.

I have to talk to Fenwick right away. He's got to find The Secret of the Golden Flower. *If that book leaves Windsor Castle...*

Chapter Twelve

"C'mon, Fenwick," Nicki said to herself, "pick up. Please pick up." But his cell was turned off again.

He must be at the castle now, waiting for everything to unfold. I've got to get to him. He's got to pull the book before they find it.

Nicki wanted to hail a cab, but there wasn't an available one to be seen. She wasn't far from the bus station, but a quick look at the schedule told her the next coach for Windsor wouldn't leave for an hour. *It will be too late by then.*

She continued trying to reach Fenwick by phone. Finally, she got through.

"I'm sorry, Miss Nicki," he said, "but I had no choice. I was with the—"

"Don't worry, I've got you now." She moved away from the lineup of people at the station. "I'll explain everything to you later, but here's the short version: I broke into Warren Letch's office, and—"

"You did what?"

"Nevermind. The name of the book is *The Secret of the Golden Flower*. And the Zidanes—there's more than one, Fenwick—are going to transfer it to that opium exporter, Osman, on Monday night."

"The Secret of the—Golden Flower?"

"Yes," said Nicki. "I overheard two agents—they must be working with the mob. I don't know their names or faces."

"Male or female?"

"Two males. Young sounding voices. They had a key for Mr. Letch's office." She took another deep breath. "Maybe they're the ones trying to frame Mr. Letch."

"Or perhaps they suspect that Letch is working for the mob and they're trying to find out what he knows about the transfer to Osman," Fenwick said. "Did you hear anything else?"

"They found a map of the English Channel. And they said something about Penzance. That's all I could make out."

"Good work, Miss Nicki. Good work, indeed," said the butler. "If Warren has some kind of intelligence that concerns the south coast, I think it's time he tells us about it. One of our senior agents had better talk to him—find out what he knows."

"Without giving anything away."

"Exactly," Fenwick confirmed.

"You'd better go and get that book, Fenwick. Before the gang has a chance to—"

"We've seen no action from the gang members whatsoever. Not yet, anyway. The tour group is visiting as we speak and I am standing outside the royal library. As soon as I find the book, I will let you know."

"Good luck," said Nicki, but the butler had already clicked off.

★   ★   ★

Anika was with Sid when Nicki arrived at Limehouse Prison; she got Nicki the necessary pass then left the two teenagers alone to talk while she took a break for coffee.

"Not very subtle, is she?" said Sid. He looked straight into Nicki's eyes and was about to say something when he started coughing—so much that he couldn't get his words out.

"I need to get out of here," he said once the fit had subsided.

Nicki didn't know what to say, so he replied for her.

"*Don't* tell me that I should have thought of that before I helped Todd."

"Okay, I won't," said Nicki.

Their eyes met for a second time, but this time Nicki held his gaze. "Why did you withdraw that money for him, Sid? Didn't you question where it came from?"

"I believed him when he said he needed it for rent!" Sid covered his face with his hands and made a groaning sound. "I should have known he'd use the cash to buy junk."

Then he didn't talk for a while, just stared at her again.

Nicki decided to ask him the obvious question—obvious, but difficult.

"Sid, do you think…is there any chance…that Todd could have set you up?"

"I don't know. I don't think so. He was afraid someone was waiting for him to make that withdrawal."

"By someone, you mean Scotland Yard, right?"

"I can't let you get involved in this, Yin," he said. "And just for the record, I am not a member of the Belden Street Gang. Never was. Never will be. The cops think I am, probably because I've been seen with them so many times." He rubbed the sides of his unshaven face. "Todd was a different guy just a few years ago."

"Sid, I think he's the one who broke into Buckingham Palace." When Sid didn't even blink an eye at her suggestion, she said, "But I guess you knew that already." Nicki thought for a minute. "Has Todd ever mentioned the name Xavier Zidane?"

"Do you have a boyfriend, Yin?"

Nicki felt the blood rush to her face. "Uh…I don't know, maybe." She and T'ai hadn't said as much, but she knew he cared for her. And the feeling was mutual.

"If you were my girlfriend, there'd be no 'I don't know, maybe.'"

"You didn't answer my question, Sid. You didn't tell me whether Todd ever mentioned Xavier Zidane."

"I like you, Yin," he said. "And I think you like me too."

"I do like you, Sid," admitted Nicki. She changed the topic by pulling out her cell phone and showing him the picture of Mr. Letch.

"Do you know this man?"

He glanced at the photograph, then shook his head. "Never seen the guy in my life." He looked up at her again. "You ask a lot of questions. Why is that?"

He started coughing, and it persisted for a full minute, so Nicki put her phone away and waited for him to control it.

He's got to get out of here soon. Real soon.

"Can a nurse give you something for that?" she asked.

He brushed back his long bangs. "They've taken a skin test. But I don't want my mother to know, okay?"

"You mean a test for TB?"

"Yes. But you see, Emma's daughter—"

"Patti," said Nicki.

"Yes, Patti." He closed his eyes and threw back his head. "God, how I miss her. She was such a bright light. She really was. That girl could make you laugh no matter what was happening in her life." He spotted Anika coming toward them and put a finger to his lips to warn Nicki.

Nicki gave Sid a little wave, and he smiled at her again, then she left mother and son to have a few minutes alone. "I'll wait outside," she told Anika.

"I won't be long."

Nicki had just made it through the front door, when her phone rang.

"Fenwick, did you find the book?"

"No, Miss Nicki, I did not. It is nowhere to be found, at least not here in the royal library. I asked the members of the royal family if they'd ever seen *The Secret of the Golden Flower*, but they don't seem to remember it."

"I guess there are so many books..."

"Exactly. It would be impossible to remember every one. Unfortunately, the older members of the royal family are in Italy right now. They might know more about Queen Victoria's books."

Nicki thought for a minute. "Are the titles from the royal collection listed somewhere?"

"I checked with the chief librarian here at Windsor, and *The Secret of the Golden Flower* is not mentioned," replied Fenwick. "He did say something interesting, though."

"He did?"

"He's just back from vacation, and apparently Sir Richard had asked to meet with him when he returned. I guess the botanist assumed the book was in the royal collection, as we did."

Nicki shook her head in frustration.

"There's something else," added the butler. "The undercover officers that have been waiting here all day agree with me that someone must have tipped off the gang leaders. The castle is closed to visitors now, and there's been no sign of them."

"Does Bobby know anything about their whereabouts?" asked Nicki.

"Apparently she's picking up nothing from Bead's cell phone now at all. She believes that he's removed the battery. You understand what this means?"

"It means he's figured out that I had his phone bugged. Which is probably why he and his pals didn't show up at Windsor Castle. They know we're on to them."

"Yes. And it means something else," Fenwick said.

"What's that?"

"It means that Todd Bead, the Belden Street Gang, and one of the most dangerous syndicates in the world are out to get you, Miss Nicki."

★　★　★

Anika walked to the bus station with Nicki, staring at the pavement beneath her feet the whole way. She grew more depressed with every visit to the prison.

"He's getting worse, you know," she said.

"What does the prison doctor say?"

"She gave him antibiotics and says he'll be fine. But you know—they treat young men from the East End as second-class citizens. Third-class if they're Bangladeshi. Especially when they're in jail."

"I hope you're wrong."

"I just wish he'd never met Todd in the first place." Anika offered Nicki a stick of gum, then took one for herself. She rolled the wrapper into a tight ball and flung it toward a trash bin. "But if it hadn't been him, it would have been someone else. In our neighborhood," she said, "every young male belongs to some sort of gang."

"Sid thought he could help Todd go straight, Anika," said Nicki, and the woman nodded.

"I know that. I do. And I have to remember that no matter what, at least I am not going through what Emma is. Losing Patti almost killed her. In fact, I think sometimes she wishes it had." She pulled a tissue out of her purse and dabbed under her eyes.

Nicki thought about her birth parents and how they must have felt when they had to give her away. Maybe they still missed her. Maybe they still worried about her. They wouldn't even know whether she was alive or dead.

The bus to Milchester rolled in, and Anika got on, but when Nicki spotted an express coach to Heathrow Airport pulling in behind, she quickly changed her plans.

"I'll see you at Emma's," she told Anika. "There's something I have to do."

Chapter Thirteen

Nicki bought a baseball cap from a souvenir stand and pulled it down over her forehead. She forced her way through the crowds at Heathrow, searching for the flower seller. Rather than approach her directly right away, Nicki's plan was to follow her around and try to glean information as to her identity.

After more than an hour, she was ready to give up. The airport was a huge place with swarms of men, women, and children moving in every direction, so it was next to impossible to find any one person. Nicki returned to the area where she had first seen the flower seller, but the woman was nowhere in sight.

She glanced at a row of boutiques that lined the eastern corridor and spotted a flower shop called Flowers Galore. Figuring the vendor might work out of that location, she browsed inside. It wasn't a large store, but the sweet-smelling bouquets and baskets were well-designed, beautiful to look at, and pricey.

A young clerk greeted her. "How can I help you?" she asked.

"I was in the airport a few days ago," said Nicki, "and a flower seller with a cart sold me a beautiful bouquet. It was like…" Nicki looked around to find something similar. "Like that one." She pointed to an arrangement that contained poppy seed pods.

"You must mean Zara."

"Does Zara have red hair?" asked Nicki.

"Yes, she does," said the clerk.

"Is she here today?" asked Nicki.

"No, I'm sorry. She works part-time," said the clerk.

Nicki thought fast. "Could I leave her a note? I wanted to thank her for the lovely flowers. My friend was delighted with them."

The clerk found a piece of paper and handed it to Nicki with a pen; she wrote down some words of thanks and gave it back. The sales clerk folded the paper in half, then put it into an envelope. "Zara Smith" she wrote on the front.

Zara Smith, thought Nicki. *Sounds like a phony last name to me.*

The door that led to a storage area had been left ajar and Nicki spotted several large cartons stacked against the wall; they were marked "Imported from Turkey." While the clerk helped other customers, Nicki continued to browse, waiting for the opportunity to get through the door and look inside the boxes.

Once the clerk's head was turned, she slipped in.

The boxes were fairly large but felt light when she picked one up. According to the courier labels they had been forwarded to the shop from Flowers Galore International with an address on the island of Jersey.

So Flowers Galore is a franchise, thought Nicki. *And it looks to be based in the Channel Islands.*

Just as she went to peel back the tape, the clerk stopped her.

"Oh, Miss," she said. "You're not supposed to be in here."

"I'd like to buy this box of flowers," said Nicki, and handed her the carton.

"I'm sorry," said the clerk. This time her tone was less friendly. "Those boxes are for the owner."

"You must think I'm terribly nosy," said Nicki, "but who owns this *Flowers Galore* store anyway?"

"I've never met the owner. Only the manager. But we've been instructed not to open any shipments whatsoever without permission."

Nicki rose early on Sunday morning and took only a short run before changing to go back into the city. Emma was still asleep, but Anika heard her and came into the kitchen.

"Where are you going?" she asked Nicki. "If you're headed to Limehouse—"

"Oh, not today, Anika. Actually, I'm going to a bookshop in Piccadilly—Talon's. But I'll be in to see Sid soon, I promise."

Anika smiled—barely.

"Thanks, Yin. Your visits have come to mean the world to him."

Nicki caught an early coach downtown, then took the tube to Piccadilly. She pulled out the business card she'd found in Letch's file, checked the address, and made her way to the shop.

A small copper sign on the side of the brick building said that the first bookstore in London had been located in that very building. The antiquarian bookshop was located on the second floor, accessed through the travel agency housed on the lower level. The two businesses were not yet open, so Nicki went around to the back and climbed up a steep flight of stairs to the second floor.

She knocked several times before a sleepy-looking man finally pulled up the blind covering a small window in the door and peered out at her.

"We don't open until noon," he said. "And this is not the entrance. You have to go through the travel agency downstairs."

The blind fell down.

"Mr. Talon?" said Nicki. "Sir, I hate to trouble you, I really do, but this is—well, this is important." She could see his silhouette in the doorway so kept on talking. "You see, it involves the royal family."

"It does?" said the bookseller.

Nicki wished she could tell him that she was associated with the SIS, but that was out of the question. She wasn't sure if the man knew that Mr. Letch was an agent or if Letch had used his real name when he obtained the business card.

"Uh, Warren…is a friend of mine and well, he's been trying to locate a book that should be in the royal collection, but it appears to be missing."

"Warren Letch?"

Okay, so he used his real name.

"Yes, yes that's right. I need your help. I know one of the butlers at the palace, and he is willing to help Mr. Letch find the book, but we need more information about it first. And I can't ask Mr. Letch about it right now—"

"I don't see what I can do," said the man.

"Mr. Talon, your expertise is very valuable. If you could tell me what you know about a certain book, one that Mr. Letch has been searching for, it could help us—"

The door opened, and the man let Nicki inside. He was in his sixties, and had his hair not been disheveled from being dragged out of bed, Nicki thought he would look quite distinguished.

He reminds me of Fenwick.

Mr. Talon pulled a housecoat over his pajamas and led Nicki through his small apartment and past double doors to the bookshop. It wasn't large, but with twelve-foot-high ceilings and sliding ladders across every row of shelves, he was able to house thousands of books.

Mr. Talon pulled out a velvet-cushioned, high-backed chair for Nicki and sat down at a huge oak desk. "What's this about Warren Letch and the royal family?" he asked. "He's a teacher of some sort, is he not?"

Okay, thought Nicki, *he has no idea that Letch is a spy.*

"Right. From what I understand, Mr. Letch attended a lecture at the Natural History Museum and has been trying to help the museum's superintendent locate a particular book, but—"

"Are you one of his students?"

"Yes, yes I am. Anyway, the book is *The Secret of the Golden Flower*. Did he ask you about it?"

"No, he didn't mention that book in particular."

"I guess he didn't have the exact title at the time," suggested Nicki.

Mr. Talon leaned back in his chair. "Mr. Letch wanted to know about Chinese books and asked if Queen Victoria had any particular books in her collection that were brought back on the HMS *Bacchante*."

"When her grandsons sailed to China," added Nicki.

"Yes, that's right." He got up and walked to the other side of the room. Then he reached for a book and pulled it out. "*The Secret of the Golden Flower*," he said. "This one never came to mind. At least not until yesterday."

"Yesterday?"

He sat back down. "Someone asked to see it."

"Really?" Nicki felt her heart racing, but stayed calm. "Who was that?"

"Oh, I really can't talk about my customers."

"No, I suppose you can't," said Nicki, still keeping it cool.

"Well, this individual wouldn't have anything to do with your situation."

"Did this person say why he—or she—was interested in the book?"

"No, and I've said enough already," declared Mr. Talon. "Anyway, he wanted an older copy, with the original Chinese characters. This one, in English, was printed in 1931."

Nicki held out her hand. "May I take a look?"

He gave her the book, and she opened it carefully. It was a slim volume and appeared to be a series of meditations. "Is it valuable at all?"

"Not particularly. The copy you hold in your hand is one of the first printings in translation, but even it wouldn't be worth more than two hundred euros." He rose again and carefully picked up an early edition of *Alice in Wonderland*. "Now this would be worth a hundred times that."

"What about an earlier copy of the *Golden Flower*, if it had been printed in China?" asked Nicki.

"It would be worth more than the translated one, but not a great deal more."

"Could you tell me a bit about *The Secret of the Golden Flower*?" Nicki was looking for anything that could explain why Zidane was after it. "It appears to be a book about meditation, am I right?"

"Yes, it is a manual of Buddhist directions for gaining strength by pulling energy inside oneself." He smiled. "Rather like the kind of strength young people might gain if they put down their cell phones once in a while. It teaches a person to be able to turn off the outside world in order to hear the tiny voice inside. The voice that has the real answers."

"I see," said Nicki. She leaned in to encourage him to tell her more.

"Essentially, it is an ancient Chinese alchemical text about the golden elixir of life." He took the book from Nicki, opened it, and paged through to refresh his memory. "Yes, it's about The Old Master, Lao Tse, and his basic premise of *wu wei*."

"Wu wei?"

"Action through non-action. Learning not to react without thought for others and for yourself—so that you are never a victim of circumstances." He smiled again. "Fascinating stuff."

It reminds me of some of the principles of kung fu, thought Nicki.

"What is the golden flower?" she asked.

"I believe the golden flower, known as *chin hua*, grows by being detached from all entanglement with the outer world. It is eternal, unlike the changing things we tend to cling to in our everyday lives."

Nicki liked what she heard. It made sense to her somewhere deep inside. But she still couldn't figure out why a drug trafficking syndicate would be interested in Chinese alchemy.

"You would think that if Queen Victoria had been given this book by Prince Albert and his brother, she would have kept it at Buckingham Palace or Windsor Castle," said Nicki. "But my friend, the butler, told me that the book is not in either library."

"And Warren Letch and the superintendent want to find it?" asked Mr. Talon.

Before the bookseller had a chance to probe further, Nicki diverted his attention. "Have you ever seen the royal library?"

"The royal library has some amazing books. Some were

printed in the eighteenth century, and there are even some very early illuminated manuscripts and a fine group of incunabula."

"There's a word I've never heard," said Nicki.

"Incunabula are the earliest and rarest Western printed books, dating from the period before 1500." He turned slightly and looked out the window behind him. "Wonderful books, that's for sure." He swung back around. "But this Chinese text—*The Secret of the Golden Flower*—is not the kind of thing to be found in the royal library." He thought for a minute. "Or Buckingham Palace, really."

Nicki hoped against hope that the antiquarian book expert could come up with some kind of an answer, but it seemed like it wasn't to be.

"Mr. Talon, I think I've kept you long enough," she said. "I am sorry to have gotten you out of bed, and I am grateful for your time." She walked to the door that led to his apartment, waiting for him to take her through.

Talon was still thinking.

"Victoria would think of a book from her grandsons as a personal thing, correct? I mean, she wouldn't look upon it in the same way as she would the other manuscripts." He scratched his head. "No, she would consider it a souvenir. Something by which she could remember her grandsons' trip to China."

"Yes, I guess that's true. But—"

"So she probably kept it on private property."

"I don't understand," said Nicki.

"Buckingham Palace and Windsor Castle are official residences of the royal family, you see. They belong to the Crown."

He smiled broadly, realizing he might have the answer as to the location of the book. "Queen Victoria spent much of her time on her privately owned estate in Scotland. Yes, if I were to take a guess, I would say she kept that book at Balmoral!"

Chapter Fourteen

Nicki leaned against the side of the building housing the book-shop and pulled out her cell to call Fenwick. She snapped it open and found a text from the butler, brief and to the point. "Q picked up message from Bead's cell. He's to be at Crown and Scepter at 11:00. Watch from distance, be careful."

I guess Bead didn't realize the phone was bugged after all, thought Nicki. She looked at her watch. *10:40. The Crown and Scepter is a few blocks from here. Probably fastest on foot.*

She deleted Fenwick's text and took off for the upscale pub she had often visited with her parents. She ran at full tilt and was there before the stroke of eleven. Once she'd caught her breath, she peered in the front window; there was no sign of Bead. Across the street she spotted a food cart and figured it would be a good place to wait and watch for the young man to arrive.

She crossed and made her way to the cart. Then she called Fenwick, to let him know she had the situation covered—and to tell him about Balmoral.

"Miss Nicki?" she heard him say.

"Fenwick, you won't believe it, but I think I know where the—"

She felt a hand grab her neck and a knife poke the center of her back. Three young men, one of them Todd Bead, surrounded her. She'd fallen into a trap.

The guy with the knife hung his arm over her shoulder to make it look like he was her boyfriend, while Bead tried to grab the phone from her hand. She twisted out from under the guy's arm and bumped into a newspaper stand.

"Miss Nicki? Are you there?" She heard Fenwick's voice coming through the phone.

"Butterfly," she said softly.

With her thumbnail she quickly slid open the panel on the bottom of the cell and pushed the self-destruct button. She squinted, expecting a loud bang or a puff of smoke. Instead, there was just a slight buzzing and several clicks.

"Oi! What are you doing?" demanded the guy with the knife. He grabbed Nicki by the arm.

"What's going on?" shouted the newspaper vendor.

"Just a little spat with the Love and Kisses," replied the guy with the knife. He lifted Nicki's ponytail and twirled it around playfully.

Nicki opened her mouth to call out but thought better of it when the thug draped his arm around her neck and flashed the knife he had up his sleeve.

"Take it somewhere else, will ya!" the vendor hollered.

"Get the phone, Bead," the third guy said. He positioned himself behind Nicki, blocking her from view as they walked away from the vendor.

Bead was walking close on the other side of Nicki. He put out his hand. "Give it to me," he said. "Now!" he hissed into her ear.

She gave him her phone. Her mind was racing. It wouldn't be difficult to disable any one of these guys, even the third one, who was tall and muscular. She could use Wing Chun defense moves—or simply make a run for it.

But then I wouldn't learn anything, she thought. *It would be better if I let these creeps lead me to their boss.*

"Keep walking," said the big one.

"You've got to watch this chick, Seth," said Bead. "She's wicked when she wants to be." *So the big guy is Seth. Thanks for the info, Todd.*

"Give me a break," said the one with the knife, who still had his arm draped tightly around Nicki's neck. "She's ninety pounds soaking wet."

How much do these guys know about me? she wondered. *Best to let them think I'm defenseless.* She was skilled at finding ways to keep control of every situation; the first rule was never to let fear overtake you.

They hustled her quickly down Regent Street, and Nicki made no attempt to break away. They led her into a small parking lot toward an older model, badly rusted car with duct tape across the windshield. They threw her into the back seat and Seth climbed in beside her. "Don't touch that door handle," he told her, "or I'll break your neck."

But Nicki had no intention of trying the door handle. She had already decided she was going along for the ride. *I can escape at any moment, but if I wait, I might get some useful intel.*

The guy with the knife got in the driver's seat, and Bead sat in the front next to him.

"Bead," said the driver as he pulled into traffic, "go through the list of contacts on her phone, then pull out the battery. We don't want the Scuffers tracking her down."

"Scuffers?" Nicki asked.

"The bottles and stoppers," sneered Seth.

"Bottles and stoppers," mumbled Nicki. "Coppers?"

"Shut up!" said the driver.

"There's nothing on this phone," said Bead. He shook it a few times. "It's wiped clean."

"Give it to me," said Seth, and Bead threw it at him.

"It's broken," said Nicki.

Seth fiddled with it, then tried making a call.

Nicki diverted his attention. *If I do nothing else, I've got to find out what they know about* The Secret of the Golden Flower.

"Look, I know you've been trying to find a book. A Chinese book."

Bead and the driver looked at each other.

"Where is it?" demanded Seth. He tossed the phone back into the front seat, grabbed a switchblade from his top pocket, and held it directly under her chin.

"If I tell you, will you give me some information in return?" she bluffed, pushing the knife away with the back of her hand.

"You're some bird, you are," declared Seth.

"Who are you working for?" asked Nicki. "Whatever they're paying you, it must be good since you don't care if Sid Jabbar is locked up. Nice way to treat one of your own. I thought folks from the East End looked out for one another."

"Enough talk!" Seth slapped her across the face. "Maybe that will finally shut you up."

For a full minute, Nicki could do nothing but try to pull back her focus. Pain was nothing new to her; she'd endured countless hits in the thousands of hours she'd trained and knew that ultimately, it was mind over matter.

She thought about her training and how well she was able to handle physical pain. *It's the other kind of pain—the emotional kind—that really hurts.* But she knew she couldn't afford the luxury of feeling sorry for herself, especially not in this situation. She focused her mind on the many things she'd learned from some of the finest martial artists in the world.

And then it hit her.

All these guys—all three of them—would have loved the chance to learn martial arts, I'm sure. But they didn't have the opportunity to train the way I did. Their only option in life was to join a gang and learn to steal and use violence to try to get some control over their lives.

"How is your treatment going, Todd?" she asked.

He swung around to blast her. "Mind your own business."

Nicki could tell by the sweat on the back of his neck that he was going to need a fix soon.

"Sid's worried about you, Todd," Nicki said. "He's sitting in jail because of you. And he's very sick. Still, he's not giving them information. That's because he's a friend—a real friend."

Seth raised his hand threateningly. "Once and for all, cut the natter," he said, "or I'll—"

"You'll what?" Nicki asked calmly. Her tone made it clear that she wasn't going to let them get the upper hand, even if he were to strike her again.

She turned and watched out the window as they pulled into an alley and parked the car.

The driver made a call. "Yeah," he said. "We've got her." He listened, nodding his head. "Chamber of Horrors, got it."

Chamber of Horrors?

Nicki looked up at the huge building behind which they were parked and realized it was the House of Wax.

Madame Tussaud's. The plastic surgeon.

"Don't get any big ideas about screaming for help," Seth threatened. "Besides, where we're taking you, no one would hear you anyway."

As the driver got out of the car, Bead, sweating more than ever from heroin withdrawal, pushed a dirty rag into her mouth. The driver yanked her out of the car, and Seth bound her arms tightly behind her.

Maybe I should take them out now, she thought. *But if I let them drag me inside the wax museum, I might be able to find out who the crooked plastic surgeon is.*

They pushed her in through the basement entrance and hurried her past dozens of wax mannequins and costumes and boxes of eyeballs and wigs into an old service elevator. It creaked and groaned under their weight, and somewhere between the third and fourth floor, the whole platform dropped a few feet down. Finally, it moved up again, then stopped. The gate-like doors grudgingly parted.

"Dr. Creen says to leave her in the Chamber of Horrors area," said the driver.

Dr. Creen! My mother's plastic surgeon!

Chapter Fifteen

Seth kept a knife under Nicki's chin while Bead and the other guy went off to find Dr. Creen. To Nicki's left stood a giant replica of Frankenstein's monster. Not far from him was Count Dracula, looking so real she could feel the teeth in her neck. The skin on her arms began to prickle and rise into goose bumps. Even Seth looked none too pleased; he never let his gaze fall for very long on any of the wax figures.

Nicki hoped for an opportunity to strike and escape before the plastic surgeon could recognize her. Ordinarily, it could be done in an instant, but with her arms tied and Seth pinning her in a cramped corner, she couldn't get enough of a swing with her legs.

"Where the hell are they?" Seth said, looking at the door that Bead and the driver had slithered through. "What's taking them so long?" Given that Nicki was gagged, she figured he wasn't looking for a reply, just some relief from the heavy feeling of doom in which this Chamber of Horrors was cloaked.

Whenever Seth let the knife drop slightly, Nicki inched imperceptibly closer to Frankenstein's monster. She planned to kick it over in the hope that it would distract Seth and she could make a run for it. But before she could do so, Bead returned with the driver—and enough heroin to last them a month.

They had also brought several yards of gauze, which they wound around Nicki's eyes. "The doctor will see you shortly," the driver said to Nicki with a sneer, "but you won't be able to see him." They all laughed and headed for the lift. She heard the creak of the elevator doors and the banging sound the lift made at each floor as it thrashed its way down to the ground level, leaving her alone to face her fate.

Standing there bound, gagged, and blindfolded, Nicki tried to think of a way to loosen or cut the cords on her arms or at least work the gauze off her eyes. She wondered if she could use part of one of the wax figures as a tool of some kind. She began to move slowly across the hardwood floor until she bumped into a body.

It didn't feel like a wax statue.

"Fu Yin," said a man. "How lovely to meet you."

That's Dr. Creen, all right. I recognize his voice.

"Have we met?" he asked, even though it was obvious she couldn't answer. She could feel his breath against her face as he examined her features.

Maybe he won't recognize me, she told herself. *It's been over a year.*

"You look very familiar," he said. "I don't forget noses, and I know that one."

He yanked down the gauze.

"Nicki Haddon!"

He pulled the blindfold back up and didn't say anything for a full minute.

"I certainly didn't expect the spy to be you. No indeed." He was silent again. Nicki could almost hear the wheels turning in his brain. "And how is your lovely mother, my dear?" he asked. "She should be scheduling another Botox treatment soon. Remind her for me, will you?" He paused, then Nicki heard a faint but definite chuckle. "Oh, I guess that will be impossible, since you will never see her again."

Nicki fought to free her arms, but couldn't budge them an inch. She tried to yell but the gag in her mouth muffled her voice to nothing but a useless murmur.

"Yes, it's too bad for your mother," he continued, "but you should have thought of that before you stuck that little nose of yours where it doesn't belong." He stroked her face with the back of his hand and Nicki jumped. "A perfect nose, I will admit. Perhaps I should make a plaster cast of it before I—"

Nicki snapped her head back.

"I'd like to see your lovely eyes once more," he said, pulling the gauze up to her forehead. Nicki blinked when the light hit her. The first face she saw was that of Jack the Ripper, his evil leering eyes staring into her own and blood dripping from the knife he used to murder and disembowel his female victims. But the Ripper in front of her was only wax. To her left was the real monster. And he had a gun.

"Your mother will be upset when she hears you've disappeared," he said, this time tracing her chin with his index finger, "but there are plenty more girls where you came from. She'll have no trouble finding another one."

Nicki could not allow his poison to take hold of her emotions, and she could not become the slave of her own fear. She had been trained to think through every situation, however dire—to compose herself and prepare a plan of action. She gained control of her focus and remembered to unwind her muscles—tense muscles are not as effective as those that are relaxed. Even though her arms were bound, she looked for holes and weaknesses in her opponent's stance and readied herself for attack.

If he's forgotten about my martial arts training, he'll let down his guard. I hope Bead didn't think to tell him.

"Come now, Miss Haddon," said Creen. He pushed the gun into her back and led her through metal doors into a sterile, white-tiled operating room. Once he shut the doors behind them, they locked automatically. Then he removed the gag from Nicki's mouth.

"Better?" he said, his voice condescending and cold.

Nicki glanced at the window, but quickly remembered she was four floors from the ground.

"You can yell, if you like," added Dr. Creen. "This floor is the Chamber of Horrors storage area. There are two floors between you and the nearest public exhibit." He laughed. "I could shoot you here and nobody would be the wiser. But I don't want that much blood."

"Is this where you alter the faces of syndicate members?" asked Nicki.

He didn't reply.

"Oh, come on. You must have done something to Xavier Zidane's features so he could cross the border—to get him past the facial recognition software."

Creen gave an exaggerated shrug. "Perhaps, Miss Haddon."

"You must truly excel at your work to be able to change someone's appearance like that. The old days of fake beards and mustaches are over, I guess." As she spoke, she inched ever so slowly toward the door.

"I do my best work in this office," bragged the surgeon. "And yes, it isn't easy. The eyebrows have to be raised or low-ered—and that kind of surgery can take weeks to heal."

"But you still have your usual patients, right?" She edged closer still.

"My regular office is full of vain women, wanting to look young forever." He sneered. "It bores me." He opened up a cupboard and pulled out a syringe. When he did, he set the gun down on the counter, watching as Nicki took a few more steps. "The door is locked, Miss Haddon, and I'm the only one who knows the code." He took a vial of pentobarbital, rolled it between the palms of his hands, then slowly filled the needle until it would hold no more.

"This won't hurt a bit," he said.

"What are you going to do after you kill me?" asked Nicki. "People will be looking for me, you know. They will track you down, Dr. Creen." She felt her heart pounding and her skin swimming in sweat.

"Oh, I'll be long gone by then." He flicked the needle. "Yes, tomorrow everything will be put in motion and I'll be on my way to an island near Fiji where I can forget about double chins and sagging cheeks for the rest of my life."

"Tomorrow night you and your friends are making some kind of a transfer to a man by the name of Osman."

"Very good, Miss Haddon."

"Why are you and everyone else so keen to get your hands on *The Secret of the Golden Flower*?" she asked. Her eyes never left the syringe, and she knew exactly where his hand was at all times. "Were you the one who discovered the title of the book, Dr. Creen?" Answering her own question, she added, "Of course you were. You poisoned Sir Richard so you could take his lecture notes, right?"

His pupils contracted until they looked like pinpricks.

"That is no concern of yours, young lady," he said, turning her around so he could reach the back of her arm. He snickered. "We'll have the book soon."

As he went to plunge the needle into her skin, she sprang into action. She pulled away from his grip and employed a swift crescent kick, flexing her foot and swinging her leg toward his head. She struck his collarbone hard and he fell to the floor with a thud, dropping the syringe. Nicki stomped on it until the fluid ran out.

There was no way out of the room, which meant that she was going to have to keep him down—immobilized and perhaps even injured. Once she was certain he couldn't grab her, she would try to find his cell phone. Whether she could dial it was yet to be seen.

"You little vixen," cried Creen, pulling himself up from the floor. "I had intended to make this painless for you. Now, you will feel everything."

He grabbed a surgical knife from a tray of instruments.

Nicki used a cross swing kick. She couldn't reach his head—he was too tall—so she hit his shoulder. The knife flew out of his hand. He thrust out his arm to stop her, leaving himself open to a vertical kick under his chin that sent him staggering backwards.

He came at her again, and this time Nicki employed a jump spin hook kick—a difficult move made virtually impossible with her arms tied behind her. But adrenaline and years of training served her well. Creen landed hard and hit his head. He was out cold.

I've got to find a phone. I'll dial with my nose, if I have to. First, I'd better get rid of his gun.

She heard footsteps in the Chamber of Horrors.

Oh, no. If I'm quiet, maybe they'll leave.

She heard voices—and they didn't belong to Bead or Seth.

That's Fenwick!

"I'm in here! Behind the metal doors!"

"Fu Yin?"

"Yes, Fenwick. It's me. I'm bound." She never took her eyes off Creen. "The plastic surgeon—Dr. Creen—he's in here with me. I can't keep him down forever—and he has a gun, Fenwick. Can you open the door from your side?"

"We'll get you out of there, Yin."

Nicki hoped the banging of the elevator meant someone had gone to get tools. Every minute felt like a hundred years. She pulled the gun off the counter with her foot and kicked it underneath a cabinet, but that wasn't going to be enough.

Dr. Creen started to move. He raised his head. Just as she went to immobilize him again, she heard the sound of a drill. They were removing the locking mechanism from the metal door.

She kept her foot flexed and ready to kick, but it wasn't necessary. Fenwick and two other men crashed into the surgical room. They had Creen in handcuffs in no time.

"Are you all right?" gasped the butler. He spotted the trays of knives and scalpels. "How on earth did you manage to immobilize him with your arms tied?" he asked, working away at the cords.

"I've had good teachers. Who are those two?" Nicki asked as she shook her arms from the loosened cords.

"Malcolm and Alisdair are palace guards and Scotland Yard detectives. They're going to take our friend here to a secure place at Buckingham until we capture Zidane."

"You mean they're putting him in a dungeon?"

Fenwick grinned. "Something like that." He looked around Dr. Creen's surgical room. "They'll pump him for information—see if he'll reveal what's happening on the south coast—but he likely won't talk."

Nicki rubbed her arms to get the blood moving again. "Without a working cell phone, I wasn't sure how long it would take you to track me down." She lifted her left foot off the ground and gave it a shake. "Handy little thing, isn't it?" she said, referring to the transmitter. "And it stays in place, too."

Chapter Sixteen

It was late in the day by the time Nicki and the butler made it to his sister's cottage. They put together a plate of sandwiches and brewed a pot of tea from tea bags they found at the back of a cupboard, then shared what information they had managed to uncover.

"Balmoral?" said Fenwick. "I suppose Mr. Talon could be right about that, but as I told you, Nicki, when I asked the royal family, they had no recollection of the book at all. I think if it was at Balmoral, someone would have seen it."

"*The Secret of the Golden Flower* is a very slim volume, Fenwick. The kind of book that could get lost on a shelf."

"Perhaps," replied the butler. But he didn't sound convinced.

"I've been wondering why the syndicate is so anxious to

get their hands on a book about Chinese alchemy," said Nicki. "There must be something either written in that book or hidden in it, Fenwick, and Sir Richard found out about it. There can be no other explanation. Mr. Talon said the book is not particularly valuable."

"Creen told you they'll have the book soon," said the butler, "and the transfer is scheduled to take place tomorrow night, so we have to get to the south coast as early as possible tomorrow."

"The south coast? So you think that's why Mr. Letch had a map of the channel?"

"Yes. A senior agent—a reliable one—got in to see Warren, and it appears that before he was incarcerated, he obtained infallible intelligence about the transfer. He pinpointed a small hotel in Penzance called The Corsair." He grinned. "It makes sense, really. Southwestern England has long been a hotspot for criminal activity. In fact, the Cornish coastal path was originally developed so that customs officers could keep their eye out for smugglers."

"How long does it take to drive there?"

"About five hours." He filled his cup. "Before we leave I have to make arrangements at Buckingham for an alternate butler," he said. "Q branch will be watching for any communication between the Zidanes. Now that we no longer have the benefit of the roving bug in Mr. Bead's phone, we have to hope that one of his friends hears from XZZ. We want to keep one step ahead of them."

"You mean Seth and the other guy? How will you gain access to their calls?"

"I had Scotland Yard arrest them at Merklen tunnel earlier today, when I realized you were in trouble. They're being held for drug possession at the moment."

"So Q has their phones?"

"For now."

Emma and Dawn came through the kitchen door.

"Will!" said Emma. "You missed our show on Thursday night. And you promised you'd be there."

"I didn't promise."

"You did."

"Didn't."

"Did."

"Oh, for heaven's sake," said Dawn, "you'd think they were six years old." She pulled some glasses from a cupboard. "Beer?" she asked.

"No thanks," said Fenwick. "I've got to be back in London this evening, and it's already…," he checked his watch, "it's already after five."

Emma looked at her brother.

"How come every time you drive out here to see me, you have to leave right away? And how come you never show up at The Coronation House to hear us play?"

"Yeah," agreed Dawn, taking a seat at the table. "How come?"

"You hate the place, don't you?" said Emma. When he didn't answer, she kept talking. "I don't blame you. I hate it too. But it's all we can get, and frankly, we're lucky to have anywhere these days." She gulped back her beer. "I mean, three middle-aged female punk rockers?"

"You guys are really good," said Nicki. "I think something will turn up for you, I really do."

Emma looked at her. "You all right? You look like you've been put in a blender or something."

"Had a bad day," replied Nicki. "I'll be fine."

"Well," said Emma, "if you're going to be driving, brother dear, I guess you'll have to settle for that herbal tea you're drinking. It must be three years old now. I bought it when I had a cold, several winters ago." She made a face. "Ginseng. Horrible stuff."

"I can give you a ride back to London," Fenwick told Dawn, but she declined.

"I'm staying over tonight. We want to iron out a few rough patches in our act," she said.

"Where's Anika?" Fenwick asked. "Isn't she rehearsing with you tonight?"

"She's with Sid," said Dawn. "They're waiting for the results of his test. If it comes back positive, they'll need to take a chest X-ray."

"Oh dear," said Fenwick.

There was a lull in the conversation, so Dawn started searching the cupboards for something to eat. "Speaking of Anika," she said, "she told me there was a telephone call for you this morning, Yin. Some woman from your school."

"A woman? From my school?" asked Nicki, glancing at Fenwick.

"Yeah. She said it was important, so Anika told her she

could find you at some bookshop in Piccadilly. Talon's was it?" She tossed a bag of pretzels onto the table. "Did she ever catch up with you?"

Nicki looked at Fenwick again. "No, she didn't."

"Oh, that's too bad," said Dawn.

It must be that flower seller! Nicki thought. *She tracked me to Talon's bookshop.*

Nicki noticed that Emma was watching her. Intently. It made her uncomfortable, but she knew the woman was thinking about her daughter.

"So Yin," Emma said, "you're sixteen?"

Before Nicki could respond, Emma said, "Look, I'm sorry for the way I acted before. I've been having a hard time, and, uh, I guess I blew my top."

"That's all right," said Nicki. "I understand. I do."

Tears started to form in the corner of Emma's eyes, and her brother leaned over and rubbed her back.

"Hang in there," he said.

"Patti's birthday is next week," Emma said softly. "She would have been seventeen." She looked at Nicki again. "When will you be seventeen?"

"I don't know."

"What do you mean, you don't know?" Emma asked. "You don't know when your birthday is?"

"No," said Nicki. "I was abandoned at birth in Guangdong Province. Left in a box by the side of the road, probably because I'm a girl. Maybe because of the one-child policy in China. Or maybe I just wasn't wanted."

No one said a word for a full minute.

"The best guess is the first of February. Somewhere in there." Nicki forced a smile. "I usually celebrate on the Chinese New Year, don't ask me why."

"You were left—in a box?" Emma's eyes never left her. "That's horrible."

Then she slapped down her beer, jumped up, and came around to Nicki's side of the table. She put her arms around her and hugged Nicki like she'd never been hugged before.

Fenwick smiled at Nicki from behind Emma's back.

Thank you, he mouthed.

Chapter Seventeen

Before he left, Fenwick gave Nicki his cell phone, then supplied her with explicit instructions: She was to meet him early the next morning, after telling Emma that she had to go away for a couple of days to a special martial arts event.

"Are you sure you won't be needing this?" asked Nicki, flipping over the phone to check for the little red button. "I didn't think I'd ever use that self-destruct mechanism, but I guess you never know."

Fenwick smiled. "Keep it for now. I'll have a replacement for you tomorrow." He turned to leave. "Now remember, I want you to wait for me at the far eastern edge of Milchester," he said. "Follow the main street as far as it will take you, past the church and the school. We will meet there."

The following morning, when Nicki was getting ready to leave, the cell phone rang.

She pulled it out quickly; it was Bobby at Q branch. The butler had advised her that he had transferred his cell to Nicki.

"Did you get something?" Nicki asked anxiously.

"Yes, I did," she said. "A coded text was sent to Seth at six thirty this morning. It came from Heathrow Airport."

"The airport? Are you sure?"

"Positive," Bobby replied. "One of our cipher experts believes it was a request of some kind, so they replied with a generic message, supposedly from Seth, saying that he wasn't available."

"And the text came from XZZ?" asked Nicki.

"Correct."

"So at least one of the Zidanes was at the airport this morning," said Nicki. "Was there any mention of Penzance?"

"Yes. That part of the communication was not in code. Then there was the request I mentioned—at least, that's what they think."

"Anything else?"

"Yes. A series of numbers," explained the agent.

"Hold on." Nicki took a pen and pad from her shoulder bag. "Give them to me, will you? I know you wouldn't want to risk texting the code—just tell me verbally."

"Are you into codes, Yin?"

"I like puzzles," she replied.

"Okay it was seven, a bracketed three, a bracketed two, and then twenty-two in brackets."

"In a straight line?"

"A horizontal line," confirmed the agent.

"How long before they break the cipher, Bobby?"

"Hard to say. Maybe an hour? How are you, by the way? I heard you had a—well, I hesitate to call it a bad day, but I guess that's what it boils down to."

"I've had better," said Nicki. "But I'm fine. I'll be in touch, but let me know if anything happens." She ended the call, headed out the door, then stopped abruptly.

The message from Heathrow, it's got to be from the flower seller! And I'll bet Zara Smith is Zara Zidane.

She pulled up the photo she'd taken of the redheaded vendor.

Good thing I sent this to Fenwick's phone, or it would have been gone for good.

"Who are you, anyway?" she said out loud. And then, remembering the woman's expensive shoes she headed downstairs, hoping Dawn was up early. As luck would have it, she was in the kitchen, putting on coffee for the others.

"I know I've asked you this before," said Nicki, "but do you mind taking another look at this photo? Try to think past the ugly clothes and imagine this woman in Fandango."

Dawn looked carefully at the picture.

"She didn't buy that dress at Fandango, I can tell you that," said the drummer.

"I think her name might be Zara Smith. Does that help?" Nicki prompted.

Dawn squinted and held the phone a few inches from her nose. "Oh yes, you could be right," she said. "Yes, her hair looks different, but I think that's Mrs. Smith."

"Can you tell me anything about her?"

"I'm just a seamstress there, Yin," she said, putting the back of her hand over her mouth to conceal a yawn. "I do alterations. I don't know much about the clients. Why do you have her photograph, anyway?"

"It's a long story," said Nicki on her way to the door.

"Where are you off to?" asked Dawn.

"Are you going to Limehouse?" Anika walked into the kitchen, rubbing her head sleepily.

"Yin's going away for a couple of days for some special training," said Emma, following behind Anika. She gave Nicki a warm smile.

Nicki returned the smile, turned to go, then stopped in the doorway.

"Dawn, are you sure you can't remember anything about Zara Smith?"

"Well, she's very rich," said the drummer. "Oh yeah—somebody told me she owns a chain of flower shops."

"How long before we reach Penzance, Fenwick?"

"We'll be there by the noon hour, I should think." The butler checked his watch. "Tell me again what you found out about this Zara woman."

"When Bobby told me that the message from XZZ came from Heathrow, it pretty much confirmed my suspicions about that flower seller, who calls herself Zara Smith. And from what Dawn says, it's possible that she not only owns the Flowers Galore store at Heathrow, but the entire franchise."

"And you're thinking she must be Xavier's wife, and XZZ is simply how they both identify themselves within the syndicate—Xavier and Zara Zidane."

"Teamwork, I suppose," said Nicki. She turned to Fenwick. "How can we find out if she and her husband own that chain? It's based in the Channel Islands."

"Channel Islands? Is that so?" said the butler.

"That would be another reason why Warren Letch had a map of the south coast and the channel," said Nicki.

"According to Warren, it's the southern tip we should be concerning ourselves with, not the islands in the channel," said the butler. "Two of our best agents are already in Penzance. I think we're heading to the right place." He thought for a minute. "Still, I'll have one of my FBI friends check out the company."

"Why FBI?"

"I like to keep prying minds out of this thing. I'd ask Bobby, but I'm keeping her busy enough as it is."

Fenwick made the call, and an American intelligence agent soon gave him the answer.

"Well," the butler said, "it looks like your sleuthing was right on the money. The head office of Flowers Galore is in the Channel Islands, all right, and it's operating as a numbered company. Zara Zidane—or Zara Smith—is not mentioned as an officer."

"But the Zidanes could be the owners, right?"

"Yes. Anonymous ones."

"Jersey is really close to France, isn't it," said Nicki.

"Yes indeed. Only about fourteen miles between them."

"Since it appears that Xavier spends a lot of time in France, it's beginning to make a lot of sense. No doubt it's easier to clear Customs in Jersey than here at Heathrow. They could be receiving the raw opium in the pods imported from Turkey, processing it into heroin on the islands, then just forwarding it on to Heathrow in the same boxes, which have already cleared Customs."

"Good thinking, Miss Nicki."

"But where does Penzance fit in?" she asked.

"I don't know," admitted Fenwick. "Perhaps that's where *The Secret of the Golden Flower* is located."

Nicki thought for a moment. "I guess the SIS can't seize the company's assets, simply for suspecting that the Zidanes are criminals," she said.

"The company is probably legitimate in every possible way," replied the butler. "Until someone catches these people with the drugs, nothing can be done."

"I wish I'd been able to look inside those boxes," said Nicki. "It's brilliant, really. What better way to avoid detection? Since the poppy seed pods would have the same scent as the gum that comes from them, sniffer dogs would be alerting the border agents to every box in shipments to Flowers Galore, right? The agents must simply ignore them."

"Yes, I can see how that might work."

Nicki leaned out the window. *Such beautiful country*, she thought, as they drove south past hundreds of acres of canola fields. "This is wonderful," she told Fenwick. "I wish I didn't have so much on my mind so I could just enjoy it."

"Comes with the work," said Fenwick with a smile. He rolled down his window to let the fresh air through, but Nicki knew his thoughts were also focused on the drug cartel.

"You know," said Nicki, leaning back into the seat, "I didn't think I'd be all that interested in learning about money laundering, but it has come in handy."

"How so?"

"I've been thinking...if Zara does own the florist franchise, she would be able to handle hundreds of money transfers in and out of places like Turkey and Afghanistan, and no one would ever think a thing of it."

"You're absolutely right. She's in the perfect position to send and receive payments through the company." He looked at Nicki. "Brilliant."

"Brilliant, maybe, but it still doesn't explain why she and Xavier are determined to find *The Secret of the Golden Flower*."

Nicki and the butler stopped talking for a while, each of them deep in thought. They drove past a series of small towns, friendly looking places with cottages and churches and family farms, surrounded by stone fences. They passed the remnants of an ancient castle; its tower, which would have once dominated the landscape, was now nothing but ruins.

Nicki decided to take another look at the numbers Bobby had relayed to her.

"What's that?" asked Fenwick, trying to read the paper in her hand.

"Bobby said the message they intercepted between XZZ and Seth's phone contained a coded section, then it referred to Penzance and a list of numbers." She read them to the butler. "What do you think the brackets are for?" she asked.

"Either negative digits, or perhaps to indicate they are subtracted from something."

"What would they be subtracted from?"

"I don't know. I leave the codes up to our team of mathematicians," said Fenwick.

"Letch told our class that the codes are often simplistic so that gang members can figure things out quickly. So perhaps XZZ sent part of the message to Seth in code because it was something they'd already discussed, something even he could figure out."

She read the numbers out loud again. "Seven, minus three, minus two, minus twenty-two. If you subtract three, then two, then twenty-two from seven, you get minus twenty. But why bother putting the numbers in a row? Why not just tell the recipient of the message to subtract twenty-seven from seven?" She shrugged. "Or simply put twenty in brackets in the first place?"

Fenwick thought for a moment. "I remember one of my colleagues told me that before the days of computers, they used to break codes by beginning with something they knew. All we know for sure is that Penzance is the place given to Seth."

"What are the GPS coordinates for Penzance?" asked Nicki. She grabbed the cell phone on the seat beside her. "Thanks for the new phone, by the way," she said. "OK, so we're looking at 50 North 05 latitude and 005 West 35 longitude."

"If we take the numbers you have there, we'd be adding seven and subtracting—what did you say those numbers were, Miss Nicki?"

Nicki took her pen and jotted down the figures. "We add seven to fifty, subtract three from five, subtract two from five, and subtract twenty-two from thirty-five. That gives us 57 North 02 and 003 West 13."

The butler mulled it over. "That would be far northeast of our destination," he mumbled. "Show me those figures, Miss Nicki." He looked at the paper she held up for him.

"Oh, no," cried the butler. "It couldn't be."

He pulled over, stopped the car, and grabbed the cell from Nicki's hand.

"What is it, Fenwick? Tell me!"

"Oh, Miss Nicki. Those are the coordinates for Balmoral Castle!"

Chapter Eighteen

Fenwick swung the car around and put his foot on the gas.

"What time is it?" he asked.

"About half past seven," said Nicki. "Can we do it?"

"If we forget about speed limits we can," declared the butler. He reached under the dashboard and pushed a button. Lights began to flash on both the front and back of the vehicle. "This will help," he said. "You'd better call Bobby."

Nicki did as directed.

Bobby didn't give her a chance to talk. "We've deciphered the message from Heathrow," she said. "Looks like XZZ wanted Seth to—"

"I know!" declared Nicki. "Those numbers that follow the word Penzance were instructing him to head to Balmoral Castle!"

"That's right," said Bobby.

"And Fenwick and I are certain that XZZ is Xavier and his wife. Her name is Zara, and she poses as a flower seller at Heathrow. You believe Xavier is still in France, right?"

"Correct."

"So with her husband in France, Seth incarcerated, and the meeting with Osman scheduled for tonight, Zara has no choice but to head up to Balmoral herself."

★ ★ ★

"I wish I had listened to you in the first place," muttered the butler, forcing down the last of a stale sandwich, purchased hastily from a roadside filling station. "To think that you were right all along…"

"I just hope we're ahead of her," replied Nicki. "Anyway, it wasn't me. It was Mr. Talon. He suggested Balmoral." She frowned. "And since we know that Zara tracked me to his store, she probably wasted no time grilling him for information about our conversation."

"Would he have told her about Balmoral?"

"He'd have no reason not to," replied Nicki. "Good thing she couldn't contact Seth this morning. She must have lost some time waiting to hear back from him and having to come up with a new plan."

"Yes, let's hope so," said Fenwick.

"But what's she going to do when she gets there?" Nicki asked. "Surely she can't just walk into the castle and start searching for the book, Fenwick."

"Balmoral's not open to the public, if that's what you mean," said the butler. "Although they do have tours of the grounds and gardens." He thought for a moment. "I don't know of one happening this afternoon. But that doesn't mean she couldn't sneak in. People are free to walk the grounds, and groups of tourists are often roaming around the place."

★　★　★

Sure enough, when they arrived at Balmoral seven exhausting hours later, there were rows of tour buses lining the parking lot of the castle. "It's so beautiful!" said Nicki as they approached the lot. "No wonder people come here to walk."

"Yes," said Fenwick. "The landscape around Queen Victoria's estate is magnificent. The grounds are extensive: twenty thousand hectares of forestry and farmland."

He pulled into a parking spot and Nicki jumped out of the car, took a deep breath of the fresh Scottish air, and stretched her legs.

"Well, we'd better get inside and start searching," she said. "It's almost three o'clock."

"At least that long drive gave our agents at Buckingham enough time to arrange everything. Remember, I'm here from the palace as a senior butler to observe the junior staff members and offer my suggestions."

"And I'm here as an apprentice gardener. Let's go. I want to start looking for the book!"

Nicki accompanied Fenwick inside, where he was greeted

by several uniformed maids. They asked Nicki to wait in the hall while they led the butler to the kitchen so he could introduce himself to the staff.

Nicki checked out her surroundings—brightly colored tartans, red carpet, and paintings in heavy gold frames. Although not as formal as Buckingham Palace or Windsor Castle, Nicki decided that Balmoral still had a distinctly royal feel, probably because of the long line of portraits staring at her from the walls.

Once it became apparent that Fenwick was going to be a long time meeting and greeting the household staff, Nicki tried to find the library herself. She made her way along the hall, but when she passed an open door to the back courtyard, someone spotted her and called out her name.

"Fu Yin?"

"Yes."

A man stood outside, pitchfork in hand. "Well, come on then," he said. "You might as well get started."

Nicki left the door ajar so she'd be able to get back inside, and followed the gardener a short distance to a large flowerbed.

"These are poppies, right?" she asked, pointing to the frilly pink and white flowers.

"Yes, of course," said the gardener. "You ought to know that." He threw her a pair of gloves that were so caked with mud, pieces of it broke off and landed on her feet.

"I wasn't certain," Nicki said, kicking the dirt off her shoes. "And your name is—?"

"Ronald. You like flowers, do you?"

"Sure," replied Nicki. "Are there more poppies on the estate?" she asked.

"No," said Ronald. "These are all our annuals, right here. We have plenty more perennial gardens. But most varieties of poppies are annuals; I have to tame them every year. They seed themselves wherever they feel like it. Or wherever the wind blows them." He pointed to the forest edge. "I like the wild-flowers. You can let them grow where they want."

"What are those people doing?" asked Nicki. A large group of men and women walked down the trail. Three chartered buses were parked nearby.

"We have wildflower walks here every Monday during the summer. One in the morning, two in the afternoon," he said, spiking his fork into the ground near the edge of the garden.

Wildflower walks. Being a florist, Zara might know about them.

"Folks come from Edinburgh, Glasgow, and even London to take part," he added.

"London?"

"Those buses are full of people who flew in from London, then had the buses waiting for them in Edinburgh."

So Zara might have flown here with these people. But where is she?

"It's a wonderful place, that's for sure," said Nicki.

"Right, then, let's get to work," said Ronald. He showed her to a potting shed, not far from the back entrance of the castle, and told her to root some geraniums. When she asked for instructions, he simply pointed to a big bag of potting soil and a jar of white powder, and left.

Well, thought Nicki, *since I haven't a clue how to do it, I think I'll go back inside and find that book before Zara has the chance.*

She peered out the window of the shed and waited for the gardener to make his way around to the front of the estate. As Nicki watched, a woman with a flame-red scarf over her head emerged from the door that Nicki had left open.

Zara Zidane! Did she find the book?

Since *The Secret of the Golden Flower* could easily fit into her purse, Nicki couldn't tell if she had found it or not. If the woman rejoined the wildflower walk, Nicki figured she'd have plenty of time to alert Fenwick and keep track of her before the buses were ready to leave again.

No such luck. Zara looked from side to side, made a bee-line to the parking lot, then ran from car to car, looking in the windows of each one.

She's looking for a car to steal! I can't let her get away!

Nicki ran from the shed and caught up to Zara just as she was starting up the engine of a blue hatchback. Zara was pulling out of the parking space, but Nicki managed to grab hold of the passenger door and swing inside. She slammed the door shut and was thrown back when Zara floored the accelerator.

"You!" shrieked Zara. "What the—"

Nicki tried to grab the wheel, but Zara swerved sharply, and Nicki was thrown into the door. The woman's purse also went flying, and Nicki spotted the book among the spilled contents. As she reached over to grab it, Zara slammed her foot on the brake and Nicki's head smashed against the dashboard.

Zara hissed, "You'll never get those seeds, you little—"

But Nicki was unable to respond. Her head felt heavy and she could no longer keep her eyes open.

Seeds...seeds. The seeds from the monk's golden poppy.

Everything began to whirl before her eyes as she lost consciousness.

Chapter Nineteen

It was the roar of helicopter rotors that woke Nicki from the deepest sleep she had ever experienced. Her limbs were heavy and she couldn't lift her head. She struggled to open her eyes, and when she finally did, she could see that she was lying on a bed inside Balmoral, and a nurse was taking her pulse and talking to a man.

"Fenwick?"

"Yes, it's me," he said. "Don't try to get up yet."

"It's seeds...Fenwick...seeds," she mumbled.

"Don't try to talk, either," he said, holding a bottle of water for her to drink. Most of it spilled down the front of her shirt, but she could feel some of the cool liquid drain down the back of her throat.

After several sips, she began to get her bearings. With the help of the nurse, she gradually raised her head, and then her back, until she was sitting up.

Nicki reached for the water bottle and this time managed to drink it herself. Lots of it. Fenwick asked the nurse if she'd mind bringing another, and she left the room. The butler waited until she was down the hall to ask Nicki some questions.

"You blacked out, Miss," said Fenwick. "You were discovered in the parking lot. What happened? I gather you found Zara?"

"Yes," said Nicki. She quickly told him about the book and the stolen car. "She drove the car so wildly, I was thrown against the dash," she explained.

"Ah," said the butler. "I figured something like that must have happened. I didn't think there'd be much of a contest between the two of you."

"How long have I been out?" asked Nicki.

The butler looked at his watch. "It's been a couple of hours now. But coming on the heels of yesterday's altercation with Dr. Creen, I felt it would be best to let you rest."

Nicki was disgusted with herself. "I can't believe I let her get away, Fenwick. And with the seeds, too." She dropped her head in frustration.

"What's this about seeds, Miss Nicki? You don't mean—"

"That's exactly what I mean," she replied. "The seeds for the golden flower."

"Hidden in the book?"

"It seems that way," she said. "And now they're probably

well on their way to the East, where they will be propagated for all the wrong reasons. And it's all my fault."

Fenwick was silent for a moment. "Are you ready to return to London?" he asked.

Nicki covered her face with her hands and sighed deeply.

"I'm ready," she said. "But I hate the thought of returning without *The Secret of the Golden Flower*."

She got up, stumbled a bit, but soon regained her balance. She looked out the window.

"What's the helicopter for?" she wondered.

"Your carriage awaits."

"For us?" asked Nicki, just as the nurse returned with the water.

"Fu Yin and I will be returning to London," Fenwick said, taking the water bottle from her. "Please give my regrets to the other staff members and assure them that I will be back shortly."

As they made their way to the helicopter, Nicki asked, "How did you explain my, uh, accident?"

"I didn't really. I simply said you were hit in the parking lot and will be seeking further medical attention in London." Fenwick had to yell over the roar of the rotors.

The pilot hopped down to make way for Fenwick, and the butler stepped into the cockpit. Nicki climbed in the other side and put on her headset. The helicopter lifted off and started for London.

Nicki adjusted her microphone. "Can you hear me?"

"Loud and clear," replied Fenwick. "How are you feeling?"

he asked, maneuvering the aircraft over the treetops and heading across the main highway.

"I'm all right," replied Nicki, rubbing the bump on the side of her head. "I'm mad at myself. I should have been more careful. I guess I'm not cut out for this kind of work after all." She looked into the storage area behind her to see if her duffel bag was there. "I guess my stuff is still in your car."

"I suppose it is," replied the butler. "Once you were with the nurse, I scrambled to obtain a helicopter. Thankfully, a member of the royal family obliged."

"Do the royals know you're an agent?" asked Nicki.

"Some of them do."

Nicki gazed down at the rugged, rocky moorland of Scotland. Had things gone as she'd hoped, it would have made for an exciting ride. But with no hope of catching Zara, her spirits were as low as they'd ever been.

"I'd forgotten that you're a licensed pilot, Fenwick," she said, "but you didn't have to go to such lengths for me. We could have driven back."

"Ah, but then we wouldn't be able to catch Mrs. Z, now would we?"

Nicki's eyes lit up. "You mean there's still time?"

Fenwick smiled. "I've contacted Bobby and brought her up to date. She's using the woman's cell phone as a GPS. It won't be as precise as the one in your shoe, but—"

"As long as it works," said Nicki.

"It works," replied Fenwick. "Thanks to the message Zara sent from Heathrow, Q branch was able to identify her wireless provider. And since cell phones mark their location and report it back to the server every few minutes, the trace can be done instantly," he explained. "You'd better call Bobby now and get Zara's most recent location. The last I heard, she was just outside London."

Nicki removed her headset and anxiously made the call. Bobby was relieved to hear she was still in one piece.

"I'll survive," hollered Nicki. "But if I don't find that woman, I'll never forgive myself for letting her get away."

Bobby gave her the coordinates of Zara's current location. "After Zara left the airport, she drove to Portsmouth and boarded a ferry. Right now, it looks as if she's on her way to Jersey."

"Where?" Nicki shouted. "Jersey?"

"That's right."

"Thanks, Bobby." Nicki ended the call and put her headset back on.

"She's in the channel," Nicki told Fenwick, "on a ferry heading to Jersey."

"Got it," said Fenwick, and adjusted his course.

Nicki had never been to the islands before. "Do the Channel Islands belong to England or France?" she asked, taking a rag and wiping some of the condensation off the window beside her. It was raining, and fog was beginning to form.

"Neither," replied the butler. "The Channel Islands were once part of Normandy, under English rule, and when the French king captured that area in the thirteenth century, the islanders chose to stay subject to the Crown of England. In return for their loyalty, the islands were allowed to retain their own government. Even today, they are not part of the UK."

"They aren't?"

"It's a complicated political situation, really. The islands are crown dependencies, or self-governing bailiwicks." The butler took a minute to look over his controls, then continued. "The Channel Islands hold the unfortunate distinction of being the only place in the British Commonwealth to have had Nazi concentration camps."

"The islands were taken over by the Germans, then."

"Yes, they were. Many of the lovely old castles were used as fortifications. Probably because they can only be reached by boat and are therefore impervious to attacks."

"So *that's* why the Zidanes have based their business there!"

"That and the very favorable tax laws," said Fenwick. "The Channel Islands are home to many wealthy Brits. It's a tax haven."

"You think those two would pay taxes?"

"On their legitimate business, the flower shops, they would. That way, they can launder their drug money and keep under the radar, so to speak." Fenwick looked at the control panel. The fuel gauge indicated his reserve was getting low.

"Miss Nicki," he said, "I hate to say it, but I am going to have to take time to refuel before too long. The pilot before me must have assumed we'd be heading straight to London."

"Oh, no!" she replied. "It'll be dark soon. If we don't find Zara now, we never will."

The butler flew the craft at top speed. Heavy rain pelted

the windshield, but he was able to navigate by using the coastline as his reference point. When he determined they were approaching Jersey, Nicki made another call to Bobby.

"You'll have to scream, Bobby. I can barely hear you. The wind is howling," cried Nicki.

"Zara turned off her phone somewhere near the port," Bobby yelled. "We think Xavier has a hideout in the area."

"Okay, thanks," yelled Nicki.

She put her headset on again. "Zara's phone is off. No doubt she makes it a habit to turn it off once she hits Jersey."

"She's been moving at breakneck speed today," said Fenwick. "I'd say she's pretty determined to get to her destination."

"Maybe she's headed to the outer islands," Nicki said. "Bobby said Xavier might have a hideout nearby."

"There are many small islands in the channel, Miss," said Fenwick. "Too many to check every one."

Nicki leaned down, scanning the waters beneath her like an eagle.

"I don't think we can find her," said Fenwick, examining his fuel gauge again. "Without a tracking device, it's a needle in a haystack."

"We can't let her give those seeds to Osman," cried Nicki. "Once they're planted in Turkey—well, we can't let it happen!"

"I agree, but we've got to land now." The butler lowered altitude and made a wide sweep as he started to circle back in the direction of Jersey.

And that's when Nicki spotted her.

"There she is, Fenwick! In that motorboat! That's her!" She took off her belt so she could get a better look. "I can see her red scarf."

The butler brought the craft down lower so they could get a positive identification.

"That's Zara," said Nicki. "She's anchoring her boat near that island." She watched carefully. "Look! There's a yacht down there, too."

Fenwick leaned over to check it out. "She's using a rowboat to reach that fort," he said. "Too many rocks for the motorboat. Thank goodness for this storm. She must not be able to hear the chopper over the wind and rain."

"We've got to land!"

"I can't land on the water, Miss Nicki, and there isn't much of a roof on the fort, just that crumbling tower," said the butler. "Is there any grass around the edge?"

Nicki surveyed the fort as Fenwick circled.

"Nothing. Just water and rocks. No wonder they like it here—they're unreachable!"

"We'll land at the Jersey airport and come back with the coast guard, Miss Nicki. I've got enough fuel to reach the airport and not a drop more."

"No, Fenwick."

"I'm afraid we have no choice."

"Yes, we do," said Nicki. She reached into the storage area behind her seat and pulled out a harness and line. "I'm going in."

Chapter Twenty

"No, Miss Nicki, I can't allow it. We have no idea who's down there, nor what kind of weapons they have."

"I've got to get those seeds, Fenwick."

With the fuel gauge near the empty mark, the butler had little time to argue when Nicki pulled the heavy harness onto her shoulders.

"It's far too big!" protested Fenwick, but Nicki carried on, tugging every belt and fastener as tight as they would go. "It'll work," she said, attaching the tether and nylon cord.

"Gloves!" hollered Fenwick. "Your hands will burn! You'll drop the rope!"

She searched frantically, but found none. Fenwick pulled off his own and threw them onto her lap. Nicki put them on, then gave a final check of the hookup and anchor point connection, while Fenwick brought the helicopter down as close as he could to the rain-drenched tower that stood in the middle of the island.

"I'm ready," said Nicki, pushing open the chopper door. She sat down, swung her legs to the outside, and checked her gear one last time. While the wet wind howled around her, she took a moment to remove her right glove and feel for the necklace that hung around her neck—her Chinese good luck charm.

Nicki stood up and pivoted 180 degrees, placed her feet squarely on the skid, flexed her knees, and pushed off as hard as she could.

The rope was slick from the rain, and she was unable to fully grip the cord, making her descent much faster than it should have been. Fenwick winced when it looked like she'd spun off the rope. Finally, when she'd almost hit the castle roof, she was able to brake the line and stop herself from a crash landing. She cleared the rappel rope through the ring, waved to Fenwick, and watched as the helicopter took off fast across the misty water of the channel.

The only way to the fort's entrance was down a crumbling flight of stairs built into a wall that led from the ramparts to the shore. Nicki would first have to jump down to the next level since the steps did not come up as far as the tower roof. She managed the jump without difficulty, but the stairs proved to be more of a challenge. Every step was a precarious one; if the ancient ledge gave way, Nicki would plunge onto the rocks that formed an impenetrable barrier around the centuries-old fort.

Slowly she edged her way. She was halfway down when

a huge chunk of stone broke away and crashed beneath her. Another piece followed that one. She plastered herself to the side of the building. Then she heard voices. She leaned over carefully to see where they came from.

Zara and two men had stepped out into the courtyard.

The one with bandages on his forehead is Zidane, Nicki reasoned. *The other one must be Osman.*

"What the—" hollered Osman.

"What was that?" Xavier looked up, but Nicki pressed herself hard against the stone where she was out of sight.

"Just falling rocks," said Zara. "I'm getting soaked." She ran back inside, and the men followed fast behind.

Nicki stayed in place a moment longer. She watched as the two boats—the motorboat and the yacht—pitched in the choppy waters. Even the rowboat, which had been pulled ashore and weighted down, looked as if it could be lost to the sea at any moment.

She managed to complete her descent, then peered through the only lit window in the structure. The room was furnished with expensive antiques and original works of art.

That's a Degas! How many people suffered from drug addiction so the Zidanes could buy that?

Nicki shook her head in disgust. She watched Zara, Xavier, and Osman raise their crystal champagne flutes. While they toasted their success, she planned her course of action.

She scanned the room until she spotted *The Secret of the Golden Flower*, perched on top of an antique liquor cabinet, not far from where the three of them stood. From the way they were acting and the smiles on their faces, it was clear they'd found the seeds.

They've probably left them inside the book, reasoned Nicki. *Poppy seeds are tiny. They wouldn't risk dropping them.* She figured they'd be heading into the kitchen for food before too long, and when they did, she would grab the book, then get back to the roof. *I hope Fenwick makes it back soon, before sunset*, she thought.

While Nicki resolved to do whatever she could to save the seeds and get them to Sir Richard for his research, she realized that if the Zidanes caught her, she would have no choice but to throw the seeds into the white-crested water.

Anything would be better than letting Osman take them to Turkey.

She waited outside the window in the pouring rain for what seemed like ages before Osman and the Zidanes finally made their way into the next room. Nicki had to act fast.

The old door creaked when she opened it and the gusty wind almost pulled it from her grip, but Nicki held tight and closed it softly behind her.

She crept across the room, grabbed the book from the cabinet, and quickly paged through for the seeds. When she saw none, she turned the book on end and looked down the spine. Sure enough, a small packet was concealed inside. Nicki tapped the cover until the package was close enough to the edge that she could pull it out, then stuffed it deep into her pocket.

Nicki was almost out the door when Zara came back into the room and spotted her. Noticing the book had been moved, the woman knew that Nicki had the seeds.

"Hey!" she screamed. "Get back here!" She grabbed a pair of scissors from the table and ran at Nicki with her fist in the air.

Nicki wheeled around, delivered a circular kick that sent the scissors flying across the room, then threw herself into a cat stance, a wushu move that balanced her weight on her back leg so her front one was ready for action. She launched short, rapid kicks so quickly and successfully that Zara didn't know what hit her. She dropped hard to the floor and writhed in pain, unable to get up. It looked to Nicki as if she'd broken her ankle. In a different situation, Nicki would have helped her; this time, she took off out the door.

The thick arms of two men pulled her back inside.

"Who is she?" demanded Xavier, but Zara was in too much agony to give a reply. She mustered four words: "Get rid of her."

Relaxing every muscle so her body remained flexible and at her command, Nicki allowed the men to hold her for a moment, in order to lull them into a false sense of their own power. Then, incorporating Lin Sil Die Dar—the kung fu principle of simultaneous attack and defense—she put herself back in control.

She pulled from their grip, and with elbows down and in front of her body, she drove two explosive vertical punches into both men's chins at once.

Osman fell, but Zidane came back at her, his eyes raging. Using a straight blast—a chain of intense punches—Nicki thrust her full weight against him and repeatedly drove her fist into his jaw. He fell back against a coffee table and hit his head on its glass surface. It shattered into pieces around him.

Back on his feet, Osman was hurtling toward her. Using the force of his own movement as leverage, Nicki threw him up and over her right shoulder.

He rose again, this time angrier than ever, and Nicki knew that it was time to utilize an emergency technique. Biu Jee is never employed except in cases of extreme danger, but Nicki had no choice. Without bending her leg, Nicki delivered a powerful swing kick to his head, followed by a close range kick, then a finger thrust to his throat. Osman fell to his knees, choking so hard he was incapacitated.

Nicki dashed out the door. The wind had settled but the rain was still pouring, so she pushed the seeds deeper into her pocket and pulled her jacket down around her hips. She looked up to the sky, but Fenwick was nowhere in sight. She couldn't go back up to the ramparts—the stairs had crumbled and a large central piece had fallen into the waves below.

The boat!

Nicki headed across the craggy shore, jumping from boulder to boulder, then untied the rope that held the craft ashore.

I'll row out to the motorboat, she thought, *then try to make my way to Jersey.*

She looked up again, wondering if Fenwick could see her, but it was getting dark, and without a beacon or even a flashlight, her only escape would be by the strength of her own two arms.

She had one foot in the boat when the first round of shots burst out behind her. Several bullets went through the side of the boat, and it began to take on water.

Nicki sprinted away from the line of fire. Over the rocks she flew, hoping to find a hiding place on the far side of the tower. Zara's broken ankle meant that she wasn't going anywhere, and Osman was still unable to get up, but Xavier Zidane had enough rage for all three of them. He chased after Nicki, firing bullets that ricocheted off the rocks along the shore.

But Nicki moved fast—much faster than he did.

Using any crevasse she could find, she managed to pull herself up to a narrow ledge on the face of the cliff. Once she had a firm footing, she visualized her next move carefully, choosing a landing spot in advance.

Waiting for Zidane to emerge from the other side of a large boulder, she listened carefully for the sound of his approach and was perfectly positioned when he finally got close enough.

Nicki jumped at him from above and delivered an incredible flying kick that knocked him off a ledge and left him unconscious.

She scrambled down the cliff to get his gun, then ran to the water's edge.

The rowboat was half submerged, leaving her no alternative but to swim out to the yacht.

But the seeds will be destroyed!

Nicki thought of the beautiful flower and the years the monk had spent developing it. The potential it held for the world of medicine would never be realized now, but she simply had no choice.

And then, at the very moment she prepared herself for the

dive, came the sound of a helicopter overhead! And another chopper!

With no place to land, the Jersey Police Tactical Unit took the same route that Nicki had, rappelling by ropes onto the ramparts.

Then five, maybe six, high-speed coast guard boats surrounded the island fort.

Through a megaphone came the voice of an officer, commanding Osman and the Zidanes to surrender. Nicki was so relieved, she slumped down onto the nearest boulder. Before long, Fenwick emerged from one of the boats and found her.

"Miss Nicki!"

"I'm all right, Fenwick. But Zara might need medical attention."

"Her husband looks as if he could use some help as well," said Fenwick, watching as the officers picked up Zidane and handcuffed him. "They've sent a team to search the head office of Flowers Galore. I suspect they will make a huge seizure of London-bound heroin in the warehouse."

"It seemed like Warren Letch was being framed, but he sure did a good job of diverting attention away from here by sending us to Penzance," said Nicki. "He must have been working for the syndicate after all."

"Actually," said Fenwick, "I called the chief while on my way to Jersey so she could have the coast guard dispatched immediately. She believes that Dr. Creen wanted Warren out of the way. He was getting too close to the truth. So Creen fed him the false lead about Penzance."

"Dr. Creen framed Mr. Letch?" Nicki thought for a minute. "Yes, I guess it wouldn't be difficult for the doctor to plant the Lanoxin. He could have paid off a pharmacist for information. But what about the two men I overhead in Mr. Letch's office?"

"We don't know, Miss. Probably rogue agents working for the syndicate. Creen must have given them the title of the book, once he had those lecture notes."

"Right," said Nicki. "And when they couldn't find out from Mr. Talon where the book was located, they searched Mr. Letch's office to see if he knew where it was."

"But he didn't, did he?" Fenwick grinned at his young recruit. "It took you to find the book, Miss Nicki. *And* the drugs."

He offered Nicki his arm, and she let the butler lead her to the coast guard boat.

"I must return *The Secret of the Golden Flower* to Balmoral," Fenwick said. Then he stopped suddenly.

"Did you—"

Nicki tapped her pocket.

"I did, Fenwick," she said. "I found the seeds."

Chapter Twenty-One

"Do I have to leave this minute?" Nicki asked Grand Master Kahana. He had flown to London to accompany her to the United States. "I'd like to say goodbye to Emma and the rest of the band." She checked her watch. "They're almost done performing for the night, and I'd love to listen a while. I'll keep a low profile."

After learning she had to leave the country, Nicki had packed her things and met the martial arts expert in a small coffee shop downtown.

"I'm sorry I have to take you away from your friends, Nicki, but it's dangerous for you to be in London right now. We might have the Zidanes and Dr. Creen behind bars, but the tentacles of their syndicate reach far and wide."

"I know, but—"

"It's better if you get out of the UK, at least for a while. Your work is important to the secret service, Nicki. As Fu Yin, you can go virtually anywhere we need you to. As Nicki Haddon, the threat of a kidnapping would tie our hands. Creen knows your real identity," he continued. "We can't risk anyone else finding out who you are. Not even your colleagues in the secret service."

His expression changed. "Although he'd never admit it, I think Warren Letch is quite impressed by your level of competence," he said with a smile.

"Impressed? I doubt it," said Nicki. "Let's just hope it changes his mind about CSIS."

The Grand Master finished the last of his green tea, then pushed his cup to the middle of the table. "Sir Richard is much better, by the way," he said. "He's anxious to get back to the museum so he can work with the genetic material you've provided. He says the seeds will germinate—apparently seeds can last hundreds of years if the conditions are right."

"I guess the monk knew that the book would keep them dry," suggested Nicki.

"Yes, the paper acted as a desiccant," said Kahana. "But I think he may have had another reason for putting the seeds in the book. *The Secret of the Golden Flower* is about living for something eternal—certainly not money from drugs."

"I wonder why Queen Victoria and the museum's directors decided to keep the seeds hidden," said Nicki.

"Opium was contentious back then—they were probably waiting for things to change."

"I guess they never really did," Nicki said.

Kahana reached for his cane and pulled himself up from his chair.

"I'll tell you what," he said, looking at his watch. "We don't need to leave for the airport for another hour. Go see your friends, and I'll come get you when it's time to leave."

"Thanks!" said Nicki. She dashed next door, threw open the hotel door, ran down the stairs that led to The Zone, and found a spot near the back of the club. The band had just finished its break, and Emma was making her way toward the stage when she spotted Nicki.

"Isn't this something, Yin?" she said. "I never thought I'd live to see the day that we'd be booked into a place like this." The look of disbelief on her face made Nicki smile. "It's unreal."

"I hope it means you'll be able to build the drop-in center," said Nicki.

"It does mean that. As the house band, we'll be here five nights a week and be paid ten times what we were getting. But here's the real kicker." She was so excited, she had to stop to get a breath. "The manager of the club told us that the owner of this place—Mr. Haddon—is making a donation to get our drop-in center started. A big one. Can you believe it?"

"That's wonderful, Emma. Really wonderful."

"Say, you haven't seen my brother here have you?" she asked, scanning the crowd.

"I was about to ask you the same thing," replied Nicki.

Emma returned to the stage, leaving Nicki to wonder where Fenwick was. *I was sure he'd be here for their opening night.*

The band was about to begin their final set for the night, when Emma made an announcement.

"We'd like to send this one out to our friend from Toronto, Fu Yin," she said. "It's one of our favorites from The Ramones." She banged out a few chords. "Let's go, ladies…"

Nicki was enjoying their fiery version of "Blitzkrieg Bop" when she felt an arm slip around her waist.

"Sid!"

"You were expecting someone else?" he asked.

"I didn't recognize you without the orange jumpsuit," she teased. *He looks really great in that dark shirt*, she thought.

"And I didn't recognize you without the ponytail and jeans," said Sid.

For once, Nicki had dressed up a little. She'd traded her running shoes for sandals and her shorts for a skirt.

"You should wear your hair down more often," he said. "You look…beautiful."

Nicki smiled.

"For a while there, I didn't think you were coming," he said. "Why are you way back here? Let me find you a table near the front," he offered.

"Oh, that's OK. I like it here," said Nicki. "How are you feeling, anyway?"

"I'm on some pretty serious meds and will be for the next six months, but I feel pretty good." He reached for Nicki's hand and smiled. "And they tell me I'm not contagious—the disease didn't progress to the second stage. If I'd been in jail much longer, it would have, I'm sure."

Nicki would have loved to have told him the role she played in capturing the Zidanes and getting him released, but the fact that he was happy was good enough for her.

"I'm glad to hear that, Sid," said Nicki. "What happens next for you? Probation?"

"Community service, and lots of it," said the young man. "But at least I'm back doing sound for the band, and now that we have a place like this—"

"It'll be a permanent job for you," said Nicki. She looked around the club. "Everyone is really enjoying the music."

"Mom wasn't sure how they'd make out in a place like this—I mean, punk rock isn't exactly for a ritzy crowd." He smiled. "At least, I didn't think it was."

"It's different. Exciting. They love it," said Nicki. "What's going on with Todd? Did he set you up, Sid?"

"I don't know. I'll probably never know," he admitted. "I think the drugs messed him up so badly that he wasn't thinking straight. Either way, I'm going to try to help him."

"You're a good friend."

"I'm hoping he'll get some help to beat the addiction, now that he's behind bars."

Sid didn't leave Nicki's side for the rest of the set. But as the band neared the end of their show and were ready to wind things down, he had to go back to the sound and lighting board.

"Be back in a minute," he said. "Wait here, okay?"

Nicki wished that she could have agreed, but she couldn't. She smiled, but she knew it might be the last time she'd ever see Sid.

She watched as the three band members lined up across the front of the stage. Emma reached for her acoustic guitar and gave the cue.

Nicki looked to the exit and saw Grand Master Kahana waiting for her outside the door. The group performed the last song of the night—which, as always, was "Tuesday at Four"—and when Emma sang about her daughter, Nicki felt tears filling her eyes. She brushed them away with the back of each hand, whispered *good luck,* and walked out the door.

"San Francisco?" asked Nicki.

"Yes, that's right," said Grand Master Kahana. "And for two reasons."

He chose a seat in the waiting area of the departure lounge, and Nicki sat down beside him. "I have no idea exactly what the CIA has in mind for you there, Nicki, but I do know that CSIS is on board, and they feel your next assignment will provide a good opportunity to learn in the field."

"Will you be there with me?" asked Nicki. "I've been waiting for my chance to train with you. I know there are some great kung fu schools in San Francisco. Maybe we could—"

"Yes, Nicki. You'll be working with some fine instructors, and I will be there to help."

"Grand Master," said Nicki, "I haven't heard from Fenwick in a couple of days. Do you know if he's still at the palace?" she asked.

"I don't know where he is, Nicki," replied Kahana, "but he's not at the palace now. I believe he's been given a new assignment."

"I wish I could have seen him before I left," she said. *I wonder why he didn't call*, she thought. *Maybe he isn't supposed to tell anyone where he's been sent.*

Nicki remembered what Kahana had said about San Francisco. "So my field training is the first reason we're going to California, but what's the other one?"

Kahana turned around in his seat so he could face her directly. "It's about your adoption, Nicki," he said quietly.

"It is?" she asked. "When you didn't say anything earlier... well, I just assumed—"

"I wanted to wait until we were on our way to the States." He looked up at the flight board and checked his watch. "You see, I had a chance to go to the orphanage from which your parents—the Haddons—adopted you."

"Did they tell you anything? Did you—"

"I found out that the story about you being abandoned is probably only that—a story."

"I wasn't left at the side of the road?"

"I don't think so. And while I haven't got all the details yet, it's beginning to look like you were taken forcibly from your birth parents."

Nicki's mouth fell open.

"You mean—you mean they didn't want to give me up?"

"That's right. A colleague of mine in China, a government official, enlightened me as to the baby trafficking that goes on in his country. Often times, the adoptive families are told that the child was abandoned, while the birth families are forced to relinquish their rights to the child. They're led to believe that the child will be looked after by the state, educated, and then returned to them. Documents are forged and the child is adopted out."

Nicki stared at the ground. "That's horrible," she said, her voice no louder than a whisper.

David Kahana nodded his head and gave her a few minutes to process what he had told her.

Finally, Nicki spoke. "All these years, I didn't think there could be anything worse than being left on the road. But being stolen from one's parents—" She stopped.

The Grand Master said nothing, but the strength of his silent presence made Nicki feel that she could deal with the news. Somehow.

"But what does this have to do with California?" she asked him.

"There's a nurse, Nicki," explained Kahana, "a nurse who worked at the orphanage when you were there. Apparently, she is the one that we have to find if we're going to learn anything at all." He pulled a piece of paper out of his jacket. "Her name is Yang Ling, and I have her last address in San Francisco. She is the woman who looked after you."

Nicki sat speechless. Her mind did cartwheels and her heart followed suit.

"I'm sorry," she said. "I didn't even thank you for everything you did for me in China. You went out of your way for me."

"What about what you did for me, Nicki? You saved my life."

A faint smile came across her lips.

"Where do we go from here?" she asked.

"My friend was able to get a look at the meager records they had for your adoption to the Haddons. Someone—maybe Yang Ling—had jotted something down about the good luck charm around your neck. Apparently it was left with you at the orphanage by your mother, and inside it you will find something."

"Inside it?" Nicki reached for the necklace and pulled the charm out from under her shirt. Checking it carefully, she found a tiny hairline crack down the middle. "I've never noticed that before!"

She used her thumbnail to gently pry it apart.

"It's a red thread."

"Yes, Nicki," said the kung fu master. "The red thread of destiny. An ancient Chinese proverb says that it connects children with their parents. And just like fate, it can become very tangled, but it will never break."

Nicki stared at the thread, tears welling in her eyes.

"Maybe your parents thought it would lead you back to them some day," Kahana said softly. The flight for San Francisco was boarding, so he stood and picked up his luggage.

Nicki closed the charm and tucked it back inside her shirt.

"Do you think it will?" she asked the Grand Master.

"I don't *think* it will," he replied. "I *know*."

Acknowledgments

I would like to give special thanks to my masterful editor, Marianne Ward, for her proficiency in shaping a story, her unique brand of polish, and her tireless enthusiasm. I also want to thank everyone at Second Story Press, especially the wonderful Kathryn Cole for her guidance and expert advice that helped me to create a young heroine who is confident, competent, and totally independent.

About the Author

Caroline Stellings is an award-winning author and illustrator. Her book *The Contest,* part of the Gutsy Girl series, won the 2009 ForeWord Book of the Year Award and was a finalist for the 2010/11 Hackmatack prize. Besides her many books for children and young adults, she is also the author of *The Nancy Drew Crookbook*, a long running series in *The Sleuth* magazine. She lives in Waterdown, Ontario.